THE TRIALS
OF THE
MINOTAUR

CLINT WESTGARD

ALSO BY CLINT WESTGARD

The Shadow Men:

    Realm of Shadows

    Council of Shadows

    Dance of Shadows

The Sojourners Cycle:

    The Forgotten

    The Apostate

    The Acolyte (forthcoming)

    The Double (forthcoming)

    The Sojourner (forthcoming)

The Maleficio Chronicles

The Devious Kind (a mystery)

Published by Lost Quarter Books
www.lostquarterbooks.com

This edition 2016

Cover image: The Minotaur, circa 515 BC. Photograph by
© Marie-Lan Nguyen / Wikimedia Commons, via
Wikimedia Commons

ISBN: 978-1-928035-04-6

For the wondrous beast in us all.

CONTENTS

ONE:

THE BLIND MINOTAUR

IT WAS IN THE FIFTH year of the rule of Auten the One-Eyed, the emperor of Rheadd during the second interregnum, that a minotaur was born to the daughter of an important patrician family, the Dethcalla. They have long had the ear of the emperor so it will surprise no one that nearly all mention of the Minotaur has been excised from the official chronicles of the day. However, a careful search of some of the more scandalous histories of the period does produce some mentions of the creature. That the creature existed cannot be doubted for, though unnamed, it is on the patrician rolls.

No one knew how Surys Dethcallen Barthil, the daughter of Barthil Dethcallan Vulgih, had come to be with child, for she was unmarried and no more than fourteen. The Dethcalla had naturally followed the correct practice at every turn in her upbringing, and her education was impeccable. To the best knowledge of the nurse and eunuch charged with her keep, she had never been on the streets of Colosi, the imperial capital, unescorted or uncovered.

Once her father, a dour and forbidding soul, discovered her state, he strove to keep the facts of her condition as obscure as possible in an effort to avoid a scandal. The girl was not seen in public company, which was not unusual, for the unmarried daughters of important patricians rarely were anyway. He had her taken to his summer estate under the cover of darkness and amid much secrecy for her to carry the pregnancy to term over the fall and winter. He left only a few of his most trusted servants to see to her care, with strict instructions and the threat of execution that they should speak to no one.

If all had gone to plan the child would have disappeared to some orphanage in one of the distant imperial provinces, never to gain knowledge of its patrician birthright, with the rest of Colosi none the wiser. The child, however, came early, while Barthil Vulgih was still attending at court, his business and duty public. The last thing he wanted to do was to draw attention by fleeing the city, so he waited until the matters were resolved and then left to dispose of the child.

By the time he arrived, three days after he had received the message, there were six census officials awaiting him at the gate to add the newborn to the patrician rolls. Though furious beyond measure, Barthil could hardly deny them entrance, for the law required that all those of noble blood be recorded on the rolls. To deny the child's existence could only result in prosecution by his enemies, one of whom had surely had a hand in engineering this predicament.

He noticed the strained and fearful glances of the servants who had been charged with his daughter's care as he passed by them to her chambers, but gave it no thought. The presence of the census notaries meant that one of them had betrayed him, so all would be fearful for their lives. The notaries allowed him a moment with his daughter and grandchild before they entered to make their record. He left them outside the door with the child's wet nurse, who would not meet his eyes.

At first he did not believe what he saw nestled in his

daughter's arms. He could see nothing of the body, for it was wrapped in swaddling, but its head defied all belief. The nose was broad and pink—a snout, in a word—while the ears extended from both sides of its head and moved of their own accord at his approach. The eyes were spread apart on either side of its face and it was covered in hair, all of it, thick and deep and brown.

Barthil Vulgih found himself trembling as he walked up beside the bed, his daughter looking sleepily up at him from where she lay. He thought perhaps this was a dream, a nightmare from which he might soon wake. The girl drew the creature closer to her breast as though to protect it, but he cursed her and tore it from her arms. He drew it up to his eyes, contemplating the now squalling beast, considering as he did so that he should put an end to the creature's life then and there, no matter the prosecution he would be forced to endure. He knew though that there was no use, there could be no erasing this stain to the family's honor.

"You are the ruin of this family," he said, though whether it was directed to the beast or his daughter was unclear. He noticed that the creature had two nubs, almost obscured by its hair atop its head, and ran a finger distractedly over one, realizing they were the beginnings of the thing's horns. Something between a sob and a roar emerged from his throat.

When he had regained his composure he carried the newborn to the door, which he threw open, startling the waiting census officials. They stared at the crying thing in Barthil Vulgih's hands with horror and then did their utmost to avoid looking at either of the beast or the patrician, occupying themselves with their official scrolls and their ink and pens. The servants refused to glance over as well, though the creature's wails grew louder and louder. The ostentatious obliviousness displayed by all those present only served to increase the rage consuming Barthil Vulgih.

One of the notaries cleared his throat, though he still would not raise his eyes from the rolls. "You confirm that the date of birth was the seventh day of Gethuj?"

"I do," Barthil Vulgih said in a voice that made all in his presence shudder.

"And the name chosen for the child?"

"It will have none."

This caused both census officials to stare at the patriarch, their mouths agape.

"It must have a name," one of them said at last. "It is on the rolls."

"It will have none," Barthil Vulgih repeated, and then turned on his heel and strode back into his daughter's chambers, flinging the door shut behind him. He paced back and forth across the room, the beast still crying in his arms, but he did not seem to notice it or his daughter, who watched him without uttering a word.

This continued for some time until one of the guards knocked at the door. When there was no answer he summoned the courage to enter, but Barthil Vulgih did not even glance at him, so lost was he in his anguished thoughts. The guard cleared his throat and then, when that too failed to draw his master's attention, he called out his name. This did rouse the patrician, who stopped on his heels and stared at the guard in fury and bewilderment.

"The census officials have left, sir," the guard said, and swallowed.

Barthil Vulgih nodded and then walked over to his daughter, returning the creature to her. "Good," he said. "I want you and your men to put to death every servant and eunuch here. One of them has betrayed me."

The guard nodded and had turned to go when the girl spoke. "I sent for them," she said.

Barthil Vulgih looked at her without emotion, as though contemplating the tithes on one of his distant and unimportant estates.

"I knew you would take him from me. Now you

cannot close your door to him. He is on the rolls, he is of this family."

Barthil Vulgih did not say anything and left the room, the guard falling in step behind him. His reply came later that day as all thirteen servants and two eunuchs were led, one by one, to his daughter's room, where they were beheaded. She did not look away from the executions, facing them with the same emotionless stare her father had fixed on her, even as the stain on the floor continued to grow. Neither would speak another word to the other the rest of their days.

•••

The Minotaur was taken from her the next day, both their cries filling the summer estate, and sent to the far end of the empire to live out its days on the derelict Guthril Estate. Surys Dethcallen was banished from Colosi and exiled from all of the Dethcalla's lands across the empire. She was accepted by a group of sibyls and their priests who worshipped on the Isle of Hizen. It was said she passed the rest of her days among them, traveling throughout the empire in her later days to spread the word of the knowledge of the sibyls.

The patriarch of Guthril was Thurir Dethcallan Drahil, a hard and bitter man, long banished to this borderland overrun by barbarians and beasts nearly as terrifying as the one delivered him by his cousin's men. That he had to suffer the indignity of housing a monster, in addition to all the disappointments he had suffered in his life, was too much to bear, especially as the thing began to walk and come underfoot. He often beat the creature with a cane, though he dared not cause undue harm. It was on the rolls after all, and there could be no doubt they were being watched by for any misstep in this regard that could be reported back to Barthil Vulgih's enemies in Colosi. Strangers were always stopping by the estate to inquire after the creature that had ruined the Dethcalla, and whether they were enemies or merely curious, care had to be taken.

In those early years of his life, a wet nurse was the Minotaur's only companion. She was a barren women, exiled to the far and distant estate as well, punishment for some misdeed that the Minotaur never did discover. In spite of her initial revulsion toward him as he suckled on her breast, she came to care for him deeply, for the world had abandoned them to all but each other. As he grew she kept him apart from the other children of the estate, even the servants' children, for they would taunt the beast mercilessly, throwing stones or beating him with sticks, sometimes at the encouragement of their parents.

Barthil Vulgih hoped that the Minotaur would meet some unfortunate end, either at the hands of marauding barbarians who raided those lands every summer, or from one of the larger beasts that were known to roam the nearby wilds. Something for which no blame could be affixed to the Dethcalla, and would allow this terrible event, which had so embarrassed their fortunes, to pass into memory and forgetfulness. Instead, the creature flourished. No matter how severe the taunts or the beatings he received, he would carry on holding his head proud and high, always keeping in his heart the fact that he was a patrician as Thurir Drahil was and as Barthil Vulgih was and would always be.

From the moment he could walk he demonstrated a prodigious strength and he soon proved to have a native intelligence to match. The nurse was the first to recognize this and she taught him to read and write, encouraging him to go to the estate's library to pass his days. He was not given any more formal education than that, but he soon had a firm understanding of the classic philosophers and mathematicians, and it was not long before he exhausted the library's supply of the histories as well.

Always robust, he grew to a massive size as he came of age. The mere sight of him caused strangers to tremble and be seized by an urge to flee. He was a creature of nightmare, the sort of beast prophets warned would come to bring ruin to lands, though no one believed in that sort of thing. And yet here he was, with curving horns that spanned an ordinary man's arms. His cloven feet left prints larger than the mountain bears that lurked in forests nearby, and his hands, though human in form, were so large as to be almost unrecognizable. His voice, which had always been deep for a child's, deepened and grew coarse as he aged to such an extent that even his common utterances resembled a man's bellow.

His childhood tormenters now kept their distance, though he enjoyed stalking them through the estate and appearing, seemingly from nowhere, to catch them heartstoppingly unawares. He never raised a hand against them as they had against him, for even then he understood that, patrician or not, such acts would not be tolerated. The laws and standards for him would be different, no matter what the rolls said.

Though he knew only too well that he was despised and feared, cast out by his own family, he still harbored a dream of returning to Colosi and claiming his birthright as a Dethcalla. His nurse had told him much of his family and the renown they had throughout the empire. The histories he had read in the library were replete with stories of his many noble ancestors who had stood beside various emperors, providing sound and wise counsel. That Barthil Vulgih was no such man, and that the Dethcalla had become something much less than what they were in Rheadd, his nurse did not say, nor did the histories make note of it.

Had she known what the Minotaur planned the nurse might have dissuaded him, told him some other tale to give him spirit during those awful years of his childhood when the world seemed turned against him. But she did not, and the dream, carefully guarded, took deep root. As he grew it began to bloom full in his mind. He resolved that, once he had come of age, he would travel to Colosi and present himself to Barthil Vulgih to claim his place in the empire.

As the Minotaur grew older Thurir Drahil grew only more embittered by the burden entrusted to him. In his childhood it had been easy to assume that such a monster, given to the care of a barren woman, could not be long for the world, especially in such a hard-bitten region. Such was not the case as he approached manhood, for the Minotaur could without doubt survive on his own in the barbarian wilds. Yet, by law, he was still a boy and could not be sent on his way.

One day, his bitterness given courage by the wine he had taken, Thurir Drahil confronted the Minotaur with his complaints. He pointed to some of the broken tile in the courtyard near the Minotaur's quarters, where the beast was resting after a day spent hunting.

"You see this place," he said. "This was a great house once. We were Dethcalla, not the cousins of such. And now you are here feasting on the coins I might put for repairs."

"It was not my choice to be here either," the creature said.

"Nor should it have been. Nor should it have been," Thurir Drahil said, and sat down wearily. "Why they chose me, though? The Gods have fated me many burdens, I suppose."

"You bear them lightly."

"What would you know of that? They weigh heavily, rest assured. But I see now that I should not be carrying them alone, as I have all these years. You shall take your part as well."

The Minotaur was silent as Thurir Drahil smiled and rose to feet. "I have a task for you. Something befitting your stature."

"I am happy to help our family in any way I can," the Minotaur said, though he feared that what the patriarch of

Guthril had planned would not be suitable work for a fellow patrician.

His suspicions were borne out the next day when a crowd of fellow patricians arrived from town for a revel and Thurir Drahil led them to the pit where the family often set dogs against each other for sport. In the pit a bear made its paces, and when the Minotaur arrived Thurir Drahil gestured for him to join it to the amusement of those gathered.

"You would not ask that of any of your sons," the Minotaur protested.

"Indeed, they are my sons."

"And my name is on the rolls, as theirs is, and yours."

"Your kin is in the pit, I think," Thurir Drahil said. "My boys have to test themselves against each other in battle to prove they are worthy of their rank. Why should you be any different?"

"That is mere wrestling," the Minotaur said. "My life stands in the balance."

"It does, it does. Some have died in the ring."

The Minotaur continued to protest halfheartedly, but he knew it was a futile prospect. Thurir Drahil was his patriarch, and while he was still nominally a boy in his home and under his care he could not refuse him in any duty. That it was unbefitting of someone on the rolls, as he knew and everyone knew, was of no consequence. He could protest to the emperor himself and the hearing would be the same.

Trembling, he lowered himself into the pit. The bear had been starved for days and was mad from hunger and the scent of human flesh that lay just beyond his reach. It roared and lumbered toward the Minotaur, who stood tentatively at the far corner of the pit, unsure of what he should do. Though he had hunted often, as any patrician boy should, he had never faced any creature more fearsome than one of the hunting dogs of the estate without a bow or sword in hand. *My death stands before me,*

11

he thought as the bear bluffed a charge.

His every instinct told him to turn tail and flee, but he stood his ground. The bear did not feint a second time and came at the Minotaur, catching him full in the face with one its paws. He fell to his back, the sight going from one eye and the taste of blood coming to his mouth. What happened next he could never recall clearly. He heard the cheers of those above him as the bear came in for the kill and an inconsolable rage took hold of him. He struck out at the animal, blow after fearsome blow, until suddenly he was no longer beneath the bear and it lay bloodied and dead at his feet. A terrible silence had descended above the pit, and when he raised his eyes triumphantly to gaze upon them he saw fear on all their faces.

Thurir Drahil, and indeed everyone, left him to his devices after the incident and the rest of his time at Guthril went peacefully. A year later, when he was of age, no one but his wet nurse came to bid him fair journey. She wept disconsolately and begged him not to go, saying that he would be treated no better in Colosi, and that at least here he had her.

"No, I must go," he told her. "Surely in Colosi where the people are civilized and cultured I will be seen for what I am. At the very least they will not set me in a pit to battle like a common slave."

Nothing she could say further would dissuade him, and he set upon his way.

•••

The journey to Colosi from Guthril was an arduous one, though it passed easily enough for the Minotaur, convinced as he was that he had embarked on a glorious quest that would end with his being inducted into the illustrious Dethcalla family, to stand at their side and be given his rights as a man. Any hardship he encountered merely fed this belief that it would end triumphantly. How many of the stories that he had read in the library of

Thurir Drahil ended in that manner: the hero beaten but unbowed, returning to the hearth of home?

He drew crowds wherever he went, though he was well used to that. Some towns denied him entry, barring the wall and throwing stones down upon him, while others welcomed him and, when they found he could speak, begged him to orate from the main square for their entertainment. If he encountered any real threat he needed only to show a bit of his sword, which was nearly as tall as a man, and the storm would quickly pass. Through it all he comforted himself with the thought of his arrival at the gates of the Dethcalla Estates, where he would present himself to his grandfather and be granted his birthright within their hallowed circle.

When he left Guthril it was winter, and by the time he arrived at the walls of Colosi spring had arrived and his coat had begun to itch and shed. It was in this state that he presented himself at the Dethcalla Estates, asking to speak with Barthil Vulgih. The general consternation with which he was received did not bother him. Though these were his family, who should have been well aware of his existence and nature, he knew from hard experience that being aware was not nearly the same as being brought face to face with the reality of his being.

He was ushered into a great hall by two servants, who kept glancing at him from the corner of their eyes with awe and fear. The hall was lined with the busts of his great and fabled ancestors, whose faces he recognized from the histories he had read. His heart raced with excitement as he realized that here, at last, his long journey was at an end. *One day,* he thought, *if I am blessed by time and the gods as these men were, I too shall have my likeness among them.*

Barthil Vulgih awaited him at the end of the hall, standing straight-backed amid some finery on a dais. There was a small fountain at its edge and he washed his hands in it before turning to face the Minotaur. A wave of his hand dismissed the servants.

"So you have come, have you? They warned me you might, but I had hoped not."

The Minotaur was taken aback by Barthil Vulgih's lack of ceremony. He had expected there to be introductions where he might present himself to the patriarch. The words had long been prepared in his head. He decided to say them anyway.

"I am the son of Surys Dethcallen Barthil, daughter of you, Barthil Dethcallan Vulgih. Though I have no names I am an on the rolls. I present myself to you, the patriarch of this family, with my sword and all that I may offer in the service of the Dethcalla."

The patriarch eyed him and then laughed bitterly as he prostrated himself on the floor. "What jest is this?"

The Minotaur, shaken, raised himself to his feet. "This is no jest. I have come for my birthright: my names and my place in this family. In return I offer you my service and whatever I may provide."

"Did Thurir Drahil put you up to this?"

"That cur did nothing of the sort. He made a sport of my life and would as soon see me dead as here."

Barthil Vulgih nodded. "A poor job he did of it, though. You were not supposed to survive those wilds. You were never to darken my hall."

The Minotaur felt as though someone had landed a dagger behind his ribs and into one of his lungs. He swallowed loudly. "Be that as it may, I have rights as a patrician and I have rights in this family and I intend to claim them, starting with my names."

Barthil Vulgih spat on the floor between them. "You shall never have a name as long as I am alive and patriarch of the Dethcalla. And forever after if such a thing is in my power."

The Minotaur found his hands were trembling. "You cannot deny my rights. I am on the rolls, just as you are."

"You will stay on the rolls. There is nothing I can do about that. And I have raised you as the law requires me;

fed and clothed and educated you. As far as I am concerned that is the extent of this family's obligation to you."

"This is an outrage."

"No," Barthil Vulgih said. "You are the outrage. I've extended more courtesy to you here than many would have. You can stamp your hooves and snort all you please, it will not change my mind."

The Minotaur could see that all was lost and so he turned to go, all the emotion and tension draining from his massive frame, which drooped at the shoulders. Before he could leave, the patriarch had these final words for him: "You are the ruin of this family. I promise that I will thwart you in whatever you set yourself to in this life. I will deny you, as you have denied the Dethcalla their proper place beside the emperor."

He was never to set foot on the family lands again.

•••

That day and those that followed he drifted around the capital, despondent, using the last of his meager coins on a little food and drink, getting what sleep he could in secluded alleys. All hope and desire were sapped from him upon hearing Barthil Vulgih's final words, along with the dream he had carefully preserved throughout his childhood of being drawn into his grandfather's embrace. With that denied…he had never conceived of such a possibility. There was nothing for him in this city with its masses of people, confused streets and shouting markets, the doors to all patrician estates barred.

He was used to stares from all who chanced upon him, so he paid no mind one day when a man dressed in flamboyantly colored robes stopped cold in the street at the sight of him and began to fall in step behind. After following at a safe distance for some time the man finally summoned what courage he possessed and approached the Minotaur, catching him by sleeve of his arm. The Minotaur glanced down, only dimly registering the man under the garish hat. He shook his arm free and made to continue down the street.

"Are you by chance the Minotaur, born of Surys Dethcallen Barthil of the Dethcallas?"

The Minotaur squinted. "There are so many of us you cannot keep them all straight?"

"Quite, quite," the man said with a loud guffaw. "No. I wanted to inquire what your business was in our fair city."

"I have no business, here or anywhere."

The man nodded gravely, tilting his hat as he did, and then leapt into his proposal. It seemed he was the head of one of one of the families that ran the contests at the pantheon. There were weekly gladiatorial competitions, to go along with the tamer sports, pitting man against man, or man against some manner of beast, in struggles that would often end in death. Most competitors were prisoners fighting for their freedom, but a beast like the Minotaur had precious few more freedoms than that in the empire, the man supposed, and perhaps even less in the way of options to make ones way in the world.

"I am of patrician blood," the Minotaur told him.

"Quite, quite. There's no doubt this sport is beneath your standing. I'm embarrassed to even propose it to you. But, if I may presume to be so bold, you seem to be at loose ends. And knowing the reputation of the illustrious Barthil Vulgih as I do, he will not have given you a fair listen when you presented yourself to him to claim your right.

"Well let me tell you," and here he shook the purse at his hip, letting the coins rattle together, "patricians always listen to this. I will give you the choice of competitor and weapons, and a share of the gates for each contest you win. You will make both our fortunes."

His instinct was to refuse the offer and storm away in a rage – that a commoner should ask this of him – but he could not deny his current state was dire. And there was no arguing that the man was right, there was little choice in the empire for him in terms of making his way. He agreed to the man's proposal, telling himself that he could always withdraw before the day of the contest arrived, and in the meantime he would have some comfort. The man, Farsyl Wyarnu, took him home that very afternoon, fed him and gave him a room in his own home until he was able to afford quarters of his own. The next day he was brought to the pantheon, where he was instructed in the nature of the contests for a fortnight.

The pantheon battles were most often contested by slaves and prisoners of war, and this was who the Minotaur was set to his paces against in those early days, though a wooden sword and shield had to be constructed to his scale first. He proved a quick study, manhandling those put before him with ease. Farsyl Wyarnu and his compatriots were excited beyond measure watching his exploits in training, telling him that he would be the finest fighter in Colosi when he stepped into the pantheon. Although he still had his doubts about joining such a profession, the idea that he might become the preeminent fighter in all the empire was not without appeal.

He found he enjoyed the camaraderie of training, the other slaves quickly coming to respect him for both his strength and the strategic insight he was able to provide them, as well as the challenge of the pantheon fight, where the goal was as much in the display provided the audience as in the dispatching of the opponent. Only in those moments alone, when the day was through and training was done, did his sadness and despair overwhelm him, which only led him to throw himself into his exercises the next day with an even greater focus. By the time the fortnight was at an end and the announcement was made by the heralds in the pantheon of his upcoming contest, all doubt about his participation had been erased in his soul. He could already envision the look on Barthil Vulgih's face as he earned triumph after triumph in the arena.

Within a year he was known across the empire as the greatest gladiator to ever set foot in the pantheon. No one man could hope to stand against him, so they began to send two and then five, all to the same end. Free men from across the empire arrived to test themselves, while others searched out the most extraordinary creatures to capture and bring to face him. None could best him and many did not survive.

The Minotaur and Farsyl Wyarnu and all his family became wealthy beyond imagining. He purchased an estate with some slaves and was able to live a life much as he had imagined during the privations of his youth. His renown in the empire was so great that other patrician families began to invite him to festivities at their estates, though none would visit his. Still, he passed easily through rooms with viziers and princes, was eyed longingly by patrician wives, and no longer had to walk the streets – instead he was carried in a litter away from the prying eyes of the plebeian crowd.

Farsyl Wyarnu's family, always a powerful voice in the politics of the lower classes, found their influence reached to the imperial court itself. Even the Minotaur could expect the ear of certain administrators in the treasury and elsewhere. The rival families at the pantheon despaired ever having any influence again and plotted assassinations against Farsyl Wyarnu and others in his entourage in hopes of tipping the scales in the pantheon. They did not dare strike against the Minotaur, though, for he was on the rolls. It was said the emperor followed his exploits and would prosecute his murderers to the full extent of the law.

For three years the Minotaur's meteoric rise continued unabated. Crowds kneeled at the sight of his passing litter. He added five concubines to the slaves he owned and was able to buy a country estate where he could go when the pantheon was not in session. The wine from his grapes drew much praise. All was right and well in his life.

The only mote in the eye was the continued refusal of Barthil Vulgih and the Dethcallas to recognize him in any way. It should not have mattered, for what could they offer him that he did not already have? Yet he could not stop the bitterness from rising in his throat at the thought. He still had no true name. In the pantheon they called him only the Minotaur, which was fine enough for that realm, but no substitute among the patricians in whose circles he now moved. One day, he swore, they would be able to deny him no longer.

•••

It was at a revel that the Minotaur first heard of the Centaur. A provincial administrator from one of the territories told him of the creature, captured beyond the border of his jurisdiction and brought under his charge to the capital. It was to compete against him when the pantheon was next in session. According to the official it had taken a dozen men to subdue it and an armed guard of twenty was kept around at all times in case it broke free of its chains.

He smiled at the Minotaur. "I will still be placing my coin on you, though."

"Would you say I have the weight of him?"

"Oh, yes," the administrator said, "by a fair margin to be sure. Of course, he has the advantage in the appendages."

They both guffawed loudly, drawing stares from the rest of those gathered.

A vizier, newly appointed by the emperor, happened to be in attendance that evening. He stood at one end of the room receiving a stream of well-wishers and supplicants. The Minotaur, noticing the crowd and having had his share of wine, decided to add his voice to chorus. As he drew closer the courtier at the vizier's side intercepted him while master looked on with palpable distaste.

"The vizier is quite busy, as you might expect," the

courtier said.

"I just wish to pay my respects like everyone."

"He does not need any words from your kind."

"I am on the rolls," the Minotaur said.

"Are you?" His sneer widened. "No patrician has ever competed in the contests to my knowledge. Your presence before him is an insult to the quality of his blood."

The Minotaur stalked away without a word in reply. The eyes of the crowd were upon him, but he did not notice. People watched him no matter the circumstance. Though he was seething, he knew there was little he could do. And what did it matter, he tried to tell himself – though they might all refuse to acknowledge his blood, even if the registry told a different tale, they could not deny his standing among them. That he had earned in the pantheon.

He took some more wine and began to feel better about the state of the evening and soon he was joking and laughing with a few of his patrician friends. They talked of the new vizier, someone mentioning that he was a friend of the Dethcalla, this being the closest someone of that family had come to the emperor's inner circle since... The rest of was left unsaid, though the thought was on everyone's faces until one of them rallied to save the day, asking the Minotaur if he had heard there was a Centaur in Colosi being prepared to face him.

It was late in the evening that a beautiful patrician approached him, the attendance at the revel having thinned considerably, and those remaining loud in their drink. She grasped him by the wrist, her slender hand unable to come close to grasping the whole of his hand.

"I am a great admirer of your feats," she told him.

"And I am a great admirer of beauty," he replied with a smile.

They spoke for a time, though to the Minotaur it seemed merely a rote conversation, each of them saying what was necessary to move their acquaintance to its logical next step. They reached that moment soon enough when a pause in their conversation stilled them both. She seized him by the wrist again and led him to one of the rooms deeper in the estate house where there were couches that they could take their pleasure on.

As they left the room he glanced over his shoulder, a premonition beckoning him, and saw a patrician watching, his face a crazed mask of rage and jealously written plain. Her husband or lover, no doubt. The Minotaur, the sting of courtier's dismissal still in his ear, could not resist a smile before returning his attention to the exquisite woman leading him away.

•••

In the following weeks the city fairly buzzed with excitement about the upcoming contest between the Minotaur and the Centaur. The talk of the match was on everyone's lips in both patrician and plebeian houses. Dozens of stories began to spread of the feats this newly fabled creature was capable of. A blow from its hooves could take the head off a man, while the grip of its forearm was so powerful it could grind rock to powder. The betting, heavily in favor of the Minotaur in the first days, was soon even.

For his part, the Minotaur felt no fear. He had faced bears, lions, even a tiger, and surely these creatures were just as deadly as this fantastical one. His training followed the same routine as always, with calisthenics of various sorts in the morning and sparring against five opponents in the afternoon. The evenings he passed at various revels, now ending the night in the arms of his new paramour, whose ardor for him had only grown after their first time together.

The days passed well, so that when the whispers began to reach his ears that his defeat was near he paid it no mind. It did engender some curiosity about the creature he was about to face, though, and so he arranged to see the beast and judge for himself. It was held in a cage in one of the subfloors of the pantheon, the only sunlight coming through the cracks in the planks of the floor above where the cage would be hoisted to release the creature to the arena. The Centaur paced the limits of its cage and its chained tether, in an endless loop, its hooves echoing loudly through the empty chamber. It did not so much as glance at the Minotaur when he arrived, though he tried to catch its eye, pacing around the cage to match the creature's path as though stalking it.

Watching the creature, the Minotaur judged that he had the advantage in both weight and reach, and, for all the talk of the creature's ability to strike with its hooves, he felt his horns would prove as useful a weapon. The previous day he had turned to the ancients, for they had written much on the nature of creatures of this sort, their temperament and capabilities, and seeing the creature now he could see the truth in what they had written. It was a fearsome creature, but then so was he. What now piqued his interest was whether the Centaur had the native intelligence of a beast, though one could not deny that the tigers and lions their cunning, or if it had the higher understanding of man.

"Centaur," he called out, determined to find out for himself. "Can you speak?"

The creature did not stir from its pacing, nor did it seem to even take note of his bellow. He tried again. "Centaur, answer me. In one week's time we will face each other in this arena. I will grant you no mercy there if you are but a wild beast, but if you are a man as I am, then I will grant you your life."

This time the Centaur did stop, though he was not facing the Minotaur. It raised its head as though testing his scent on the air, while looking at him from the corner of its eye. Its face, more human in its features than his own, was expressionless, its eyes displaying no emotion.

The Minotaur laughed. "Then it is decided, beast – it

shall be a duel to the death."

He received no response, although the Centaur did not resume its pacing until the Minotaur had left the chamber. As his palanquin carried him home he formulated a plan for how to deal with the creature. From his confrontation there could be little doubt that the creature was of a higher intelligence, not some mere beast, but it was uncivilized. Whatever strength and ferocity it gained from being wild and untamed it would lose in the training and the strategy the Minotaur could bring to bear.

When they arrived at his home one of the carriers told him they had been followed on their way from the arena. No doubt one of Jyal Iospyd's men, he thought. It was not uncommon for his rivals to follow him in the days leading up to a contest to see what he was about, and the man would certainly want to know what had transpired between he and the Centaur. He thanked the carrier and dismissed him, giving the incident no further thought, and called on his slaves to prepare him for that evening's revel.

•••

Later, in the far depths of the night, the day itself drawing near, he cradled his patrician lover in his broad arms, both of them having slaked their thirst for the moment. They could just hear those carrying on the revel from the couch where they lay, the sounds oddly dissociated from form and being in the darkness. One voice grew loud as it passed by the door to the chamber they had sequestered themselves in.

"He will see his downfall soon enough." A reply followed, indistinct and muffled, the pair having already passed down the hall.

The woman in his arms stiffened at those words. He glanced down at her and she said to him, "That was my husband. He was speaking of you, no doubt."

"No doubt," the Minotaur said, kissing her ear. "Many are saying the same thing."

"He has his reasons. He is a cousin of the Dethcalla, you know."

He resisted the urge to laugh, for her tone was serious, but his glee was overwhelming. Here at last was his final triumph against the Dethcalla. Not only had he gained more renown than they in the empire, but he had made a cuckold of one of theirs. He smiled to himself and held the woman closer to him.

"Do you think you can defeat the Centaur?"

"I met him today," he told her.

"What did you think?"

He shrugged. "Perhaps I am too civilized. Perhaps his savagery will overwhelm me."

The next day he twisted his knee training at his estate, which concerned Farsyl Wyarnu enough to call a physician in to look at it, though the Minotaur waved it away. The doctor advised him to keep his weight off it as much as possible for the next day or so, which meant limiting his training. The Minotaur argued with the physician but Farsyl Wyarnu took the doctor's side, insisting that his friend heed the expert's advice.

"No sense taking such a risk this near the competition," he told the Minotaur.

"You are worried," the Minotaur replied with a laugh. "This beast has you worried."

"No," Farsyl Wyarnu said, "No. Merely cautious. Why tempt fate, after all."

The Minotaur relented and put aside training for two days. Bored and exasperated that his routine had been disrupted, he took to his palanquin, wandering the city to no purpose for hours at a time. Each time they returned to the estate his carriers reported that he had been followed.

Meanwhile, anticipation for the upcoming match continued to grow throughout Colosi, reaching a frenzy never before seen for one of the contests. The patrician sections were all spoken for, while some plebeians had begun to sleep outside the pantheon to ensure they would gain entrance the day of the event. Rumors were everywhere that the emperor himself would attend.

Two days before the contest was set to take place, Farsyl Wyarnu came to see him to confirm that all was well. They shared a glass of wine to his success and that afternoon in the pantheon the heralds announced to those gathered that the match was set and that neither combatant could withdraw without forfeiting the contest.

•••

The Minotaur awoke that night to the clamor of shouting men rushing towards him. There were two swords at his throat and another at his heart by the time he managed to rouse himself and shake the sleep from his eyes. He stared at them stupidly, as if unsure of their purpose, while someone from the doorway ordered him clapped in irons.

While this was done the same man said, "I have a signed imperial order for your arrest. You are to appear before a judge at once to determine your fate."

Next his eyes were bound and a sword pressed into his back, staying there as he stumbled to his feet. The officer called the men to order and they proceeded through the house. The sounds of it being ransacked by the remainder of the guard penetrated his stupor and roused his anger. A woman began to scream as they crossed the courtyard to the mansion's entrance, which meant the guard had found the concubine's quarters. He trembled with a growing rage and tested the strength of the chains linking his two hands.

"Don't bother thinking about it," the captain said to him, sounding near enough to reach, "I have archers on the walkways. You'll be dead before you even get your hands around my neck."

"Still time enough to kill you," the Minotaur replied, his voice still rasping with sleep.

"Maybe. Maybe not. Now, well, consider that we're doing you a favor. It's not like you would survive the contest."

"No one has ever come near defeating me." The Minotaur could almost see the other shrugging in reply.

As they walked up the steps out of the courtyard to the entrance of his estate, he felt what could only be blood, warm on his bare hoof. The realization chilled him, for this was a different game than the one he thought was being played. If they were killing the slaves, including the women, then all his property was forfeit. Up to that moment he had assumed that Jyal Iospyd had bought off a judge with the hopes of having him forfeit the contest, but it was clear that someone else had perpetrated this conspiracy and his very life was now in the balance.

He was marched through the empty streets, shivering a bit from the late evening chill. They led him on a dizzying route, not halting until the sun began to rise, its heat seeping a bit into his bones. He was taken into what he thought was one of the imperial prisons, though he couldn't be sure. They left him in a foul-smelling place, the floor damp and the walls covered with some kind of rotting growth.

As he began to contemplate a means of escape, the door burst open and dozens of feet marched in, taking up positions around him. A tendril of fear crept through his stomach and tickled at his throat. There was a sharp word from the captain and the soldiers proceeded to beat him with the flat of their blades. This time he did try to resist, but they managed to knock him off his feet before he could break free of the irons, and once on the ground the flurry of their blows would not allow him to rise.

At some point, in the midst of it all, he drifted from consciousness, a small mercy. Sometime later they slapped him awake and removed his blindfold. The room was lit by two torches, both near him, so that he was bathed in light while the soldiers who stood around him were in shadows. A judge stood before him, within the circle of light, looking him over as though he were an uninteresting specimen, a mere criminal to be processed.

He read from a scroll in a drab monotone, at odds with his aristocratic bearing, declaring that an investigation had occurred and the Minotaur had been found guilty of various offenses against the empire. Among these were treason, conspiracy to harm the imperial person, heresy and consorting with patricians.

"I am in the registry," he said.

The judge paused in his recitation and raised his eyes from the scroll. "Patricians do not compete in the pantheon. And there is no record of your name on the rolls."

"Regardless," the Minotaur said, summoning all the pride he could to his voice, "I am on the rolls. My mother is Surys Dethcallen Barthil, daughter of Barthil Dethcallan Vulgih."

The judge parsed amongst the scrolls in his hand, an act, the Minotaur realized immediately, for his benefit. The words he was about to say had been determined long before this meeting.

"Surys Dethcallen Barthil, daughter of Barthil Dethcallan Vulgih, did have a son, and that son is on the registry. No name was given it."

"That was because of Barthil Vulgih. He has refused to give me my name, even after I came of age and pledged myself to the Dethcalla."

"He has been interviewed by this office and denies that you are his daughter's son. His daughter is with the sibyls on the Isle of Hizen and no longer concerns herself with the affairs of this world." The judge smiled before continuing, "And no other witnesses remain from the day the child was entered on the rolls."

The Minotaur felt his mouth go dry and the air leave his lungs. "I was raised at the Guthril estate of the Dethcalla. Thurir Drahil and many others can vouch for who I am."

"Sadly, the Guthril estate was overrun by barbarians

some weeks ago. It appears no one survived the calamity. There is no one to confirm your tale."

The Minotaur wanted to weep hearing that, but he held his tears in check. He would not give Barthil Vulgih that.

The judge had returned to his scroll and his recitation: "The penalty for your crimes is death. However, in light of your popularity and your service to the pantheon, I have decided to grant mercy in this case. You shall be blinded and exiled from all imperial territories. You have one day to leave the imperial city and a fortnight to leave the territories. Should you be found within those borders after the allotted time you will be put to death."

Having read the scroll, the judge turned and left the room before the Minotaur could even summon a response. He watched helplessly as two new figures emerged from the shadows.

•••

They threw him into the streets, blood still streaming from his eyes. One of his horns ached as well, and he assumed it had been broken during the beatings. Movement was agony, so he simply lay where he was, listening to the ebb and flow of the street around him. He heard the shuffling of feet, the groaning of cart wheels, and the grunting of animals. There was a low murmur of consternation, so he knew there were onlookers. They must recognize him, he thought, yet no one did anything.

He lay there for what seemed hours, his mind stained with the apathetic, smirking face of the judge. Every so often he would see the dagger approaching and then the blackness would explode upon him anew and he would be unable to think at all.

When arms grasped him he did not resist, stumbling to his feet. He was dragged to a palanquin, which began to move as soon as he was within. Every footstep of the carriers was a small agony, set atop the overwhelming hurt and ache until the weight was unbearable. He longed for his other senses to go dark as his eyes, but he was allowed no such mercy.

It was only when the woman spoke that he realized he was not alone.

"I know people who will get you to the borders. From there…" she said.

"Who are you?" His voice did not sound his own.

There was a long pause. "Your mother."

She continued to speak, explaining how the transport she had arranged would work. "The sibyls have people in every town between here and the barbarian lands, so you can hide with them as you go. I've arranged for guides to take you along the way."

He barely listened, trying to imagine how she looked. How long had she been in Colosi, he wondered, and how had she known this would befall him?

"You must be careful," she said. "My father doesn't intend you to make it into exile."

He could think of nothing to say in reply, all the questions he had once wanted to give voice to evaporated from his mind. How strange, he thought, that she should be the one to save him now, when in his childhood he had raged against her for abandoning him to Guthril's cruel existence. She was too late, he thought, and began to weep.

"I'm sorry I cannot do more," she said after some time. "If my father knew I was in Colosi again it would mean both our deaths. The sibyls will get you out of Rheadd, then you will have to find your own way in the world."

Those were her final words to him. Some time later the palanquin halted and her skirt brushed against his leg as she exited.

As they continued on whatever path she had set the carriers, he lost himself in a reverie where he stood at the centre of a massive pantheon, so large its upper reaches disappeared into clouds that swirled overhead. A Centaur pranced at the opposite end of the arena. The horn sounded and he went to move toward his adversary, but instead he fell into the sand, thrashing madly. The clouds, the stadium and its hordes disappeared, leaving only blackness and the sound of the Centaur's footsteps approaching.

The palanquin reached its destination in the midst of this nightmare and he was seized again and carried into a building, where he was left him sprawled on the floor. He tried to stand, wanting to ask the carriers what was to happen next, as he was unable to remember his mother's plan. It was a cramped hovel, though, and he cracked his head on the ceiling as he rose, falling back to the floor.

He called out but no one answered. Few sounds from the outside world reached him, beyond the chatter of some birds just outside the hovel. Wherever he was, he decided it must be outside the city walls, though he could not remember the palanquin passing through one of the gates. For all he knew they could have gone in circles, ending up back at the prison where he was to languish for what remained of his days.

He was left alone through the heat of the afternoon, with only some rancid fruit that did little more than attract flies. He slept fitfully, terrified that the stinking dirt floor would be where he met his end. In the evening, the girl with the bird came.

•••

The bird could talk as a man did, and it would not cease in its ramblings as they fled Colosi. Had he not been so weak and broken, the Minotaur would have seized it by the neck and ended its miserable life. It had begun its incessant chatter from the moment the two had arrived in the hovel.

"Beast is broken," the bird said, for what must have been the tenth time. He imagined it as a crow or a raven, all black plumage and devious eyes.

"Hush," the girl said to it in her plebeian accent. He could hear the creature ruffling its feathers on her shoulder in response.

While the bird prattled on variations of the same statement, the girl had remained silent more or less, whether from kindness or indifference he could not say. She had arrived without ceremony to find him lost in the fever of agony his still-bleeding eyes had him under. After nudging him with her sandal to see that he was still alive, she told him that she was to be his guide and that they would be leaving at nightfall. He had cursed her and said he did not have the strength for any journey and she had left. Just when he had started to believe that she had in fact abandoned him, she returned and fed him some gruel she had bought somewhere.

She had not said a word since, except to tell him when they were nearing an obstacle where he needed to take care, or to silence the bird. It seemed impossible to him that she, a plebeian of the worst sort by the sound of her voice, could be the savior his mother had arranged. Yet she had been true to her word thus far, and it was not as though he could make his way on his own.

Part of him had wished he had simply been left on that street in Colosi to bleed out or be taken by the imperial guard and executed the next morning. Better to end this now than to persist in misery, which seemed all that could be left for him in this world. He wanted nothing to do with this life so marked by desolation, the futility of his dreams laid bare. That he had thought he could stand against the Dethcalla, his very existence a mockery to them, and with all that they had at hand to destroy him, had been the very height of hubris. Nothing remained now but empty days, and then only if he reached exile, which seemed a dubious proposition given his condition.

Each step seemed like a leap off a crumbling precipice. He had lost count of the number of times he had stumbled and fallen. To her credit, the girl never relinquished her hold on his hand, though he moaned and cursed her and his feebleness, the bird nattering on. He could see, in his mind's eye, the thing laughing at him and the girl raising a finger to her lips to shush it, trying to hold back her laughter as well.

Empty and sightless days, this was all that was left to him. This was now every day. His mind was a flurry of images, disconnected from his thoughts, overwhelming them. Each sound – the stirring of the branches in the trees, the sound of their feet on the path, or the rustle of insects – sparked all manner of color and form in his mind, dissolving and reforming at every instant. If he focused on a sound, any sensation – the infernal bird, for instance – he could force his mind to shape it, to see it. But everything else, there was too much sensation and not enough.

"Not a beast of burden, burdensome beast," the bird cackled.

He cursed it, cursed them both, and cursed the Centaur, the Dethcalla, Barthil Vulgih and Thurir Drahil and his mother too. His words rang loud in the night, leaving a stillness in their wake. He sobbed in spite of himself, pus and blood and tears intermingling and flowing down his cheeks.

"How much farther?" he asked when he could stand the silence no longer.

He could feel her shrugging her shoulders through the hand that was cradled in his massive one. "It will take us most of the evening to get to the river."

What river they were heading towards and what happened after they reached it was left unstated.

After some time the girl spoke again. "You needn't worry. I meet my bargains."

When they reached their destination the girl halted and then cooed softly into the darkness. After a time someone responded and she took the Minotaur by the hand again and led him forward. They made their way down into the river valley, branches scratching at his face and shoulders as they went. Somehow he kept his feet under him, in spite of the uneven ground, the sound of the river coming to his ears as ground leveled. They halted and the girl whispered a greeting, receiving one in return. The man who replied had a harsh voice, given to whispering, and he sounded very near.

"This is your passage," the girl said. The man grunted in return and then the girl's hand was gone, replaced by his hard, callused one. The Minotaur was led forward onto a small dock and then eased into a waiting boat. He sat down gratefully on the bench, exhaling more loudly than he had intended. The boat rocked gently as the man climbed in and then pushed off. He could hear the paddles dipping in and out of the water and the river's calm passage; otherwise there was silence. Only the sluggish water beneath them seemed to be moving. He could feel its slight pull as the man worked the paddles, dragging the boat across to the river's far side and what awaited him there.

TWO:

THE ORACLE'S MORTIFICATION

THE MINOTAUR WAS NEVER to return to Colosi again. After his flight from the empire, assisted by the sibyls of Hizen, he wandered aimlessly for a time in those barbarian lands so feared throughout the empire. He stayed clear of any towns and off any roads, remaining hidden in the wild lands, forested and mountainous, that the barbarians spoke of with awe and fear, for it was said they were inhabited with spirits and monsters. At last, tired of his wandering, and having no other place that he wished to go, he settled in a large cave. Its darkness, he felt, suited one who would pass his existence in obscurity forever more.

At first he would leave the cave daily to forage in the nearby wilds for what food he could find, mostly roots and berries, but as the seasons turned to autumn and then winter he rarely strayed outside his makeshift home. He ate less and less, growing so thin that his ribs showed through his coat, which had a ragged winter growth. He cared little, for it seemed to him inevitable that he would die here, and he saw no need to prolong this terrible misery. Instead, he feverishly plotted his revenge against Barthil Vulgih and those of his family who had conspired against him, imagining his triumphant return to Colosi to face his accusers on the sands of the pantheon.

Such dreaming was made all the worse for the fact that he knew such a thing could never happen. His life there was gone, replaced by this damp and miserable place. Still, it gave comfort to the long, solitary days while hunger gnawed at his belly and mind. Soon enough, he imagined, he would be free of this realm, taken across that final river to the underworld where he would pass all eternity. That release was not to be granted him yet, though.

In the months that he spent in his cave, the Minotaur had not escaped the notice of local barbarians. Hunters were often seeking game in those forests and more than a few caught a glimpse of this strange beast, whose miraculous appearance they reported to their villages as proof of the place's mystical powers. A few even trailed him back to his cave, a place that, unbeknownst to the Minotaur, was already considered a holy place of great power. As knowledge of presence spread among the barbarians they began to bring offerings to the mouth of the cave, especially if their hunt had been successful. It was felt, even among those who did not give much credence to these things, that good hunting would come to those who made whatever spirit inhabited the cave happy.

Little did they know that nothing could have mended the Minotaur's heart at that time, so deep and absolute was his sorrow. He heard the coming and going of the hunters, their whispered invocations as they left their offering, but it never occurred to him to show himself to them. He did avail himself of their offerings, drinking the cups of wine and the hearts and tongues of the beasts they had killed. This only served to add to the power they ascribed him. By winter's end even barbarians who did not hunt in the area began to make the journey to the cave to leave an offering to ensure that he was not angered.

As word of his imagined dominion spread, mystics and other sorts who claimed to have been touched by the barbarian gods began to journey to the cave to prostrate themselves there, chanting prayers and singing songs to his glory. None of these he understood, for the harsh barbarian tongue was unfamiliar to him. He ignored these penitents as best he could, slipping out of the cave under the cover of darkness to take the offerings and then retreating back within his claimed realm to feast. Few of those who came to make offerings had seen him, but the stories of his fearsome size from those who had were enough to engender awe.

Inevitably, one of the penitents summoned the courage to confront the god of the cave. He was from a nearby village and was said, by those who lived there, to have been touched by the gods, for he often had fits and fainting spells where he would rave madly in some tongue no one understood. The villagers called him Velthar the Sufferer and they feared him, unsure whether he was possessed by some demon come to torment them or a messenger of the greater path. He had no such doubts, and when he heard of the creature in the cave that had brought such prosperity to those hunters who had made offerings this past winter, he went to there to chant and pray with the other penitents. Unlike those others, who came with offerings and paid their obeisance for a few days and then went on their way, he stayed on, praying and offering himself and his undying service to the being hidden within.

Weeks he stayed, and still he received no sign that the creature was even aware of his existence. His faith was strong, though, and he remained, subsisting on what the forest offered, never once tempted by the many offerings left for the Minotaur. One night, as he lay awake, unable to sleep, just above the mouth of the cave, he saw through the branches of the trees above him a shadow pass over the moon, blotting it from the sky. He watched, wondering if he were witnessing the end of all times, the sky growing dark, casting a shadow across all the lands in existence. Even as the darkness seemed absolute the shadow passed on and the moon gradually reappeared and he understood that it was a sign from the god within the cave intended for him alone.

Without hesitating, he rose to his feet and entered the cave and was swallowed by the darkness within. He went slowly, crawling on his hands and knees, both to demonstrate his servility to the god and because he could not otherwise know where he was going. The floor of the cave was damp and cool, the smell of moss and earth heavy in his nostrils. At last he sensed the passage opening up into a deep cavern, which seemed to him as though it had been untouched for untold ages. Here he felt the presence of the creature, could smell it, in fact – a mixture of damp hair and the rotten breath of one who had been eating raw meat. He imagined that he could make out where the creature slumbered and he faced it crouched as he was, not daring to come any nearer. There he remained through the night.

The Minotaur had heard the man's scuffling approach into the cavern, but he did not stir from where he lay, waiting to see what he would do. It had been, he knew, inevitable that one of the barbarians should at last gain the courage to confront him. His only hope lay in the fact that in the darkness of the cave the man would not realize his blind state and the advantage he held. When the barbarian did nothing, staying crouched where he was at the cavern's opening, the Minotaur was not sure what to think. Was he blocking the way, preparing himself for the battle to come? The Minotaur could only assume this was the case, that here at last was a barbarian brave enough to confront the creature who was terrorizing the land and demanding such sacrifices as they were giving him. He had only known fear in his dealings with others, so it never occurred to him that the barbarians might be worshipping him.

Now that they had sent a champion to strike him down, he both feared and welcomed it. Here was the ending that he had longed for through that long winter, and yet now that it had at last arrived he found he no longer wished to perish. The force of life had returned to his heart. As meager and pathetic as this existence was, living upon the sufferance of these savages, it was not something he was willing to surrender. So he decided to await for this protector of the barbarians to launch his attack. The darkness would be his ally and he would make this man come to him.

Morning came with neither of them having slept, the barbarian awaiting a sign from his chosen god, the Minotaur expecting an attack and a battle to the death. The Minotaur was the first to rise, the old wounds he had suffered in the pantheon and at the hands of the imperial guard aching from too long spent on the cold and damp stone of the cave. He rose to his feet with the slightest of grunts and then moved silently deeper into the cavern, where the stone formed a pool filled with water that came dripping from above. He drank his fill there and then went deeper yet into the darkness to relieve himself.

When he returned, the barbarian was speaking. He had not, as near as the Minotaur could judge, moved from where he had lain the entire night. He had raised himself to his knees and was repeating the same group of phrases again and again, almost in a song. The Minotaur listened for some time, not moving, and then realized that the man was praying. Was he praying for strength, for his gods to aid him in the battle to come, or was he in fact praying to him? Was he a god to these savages? The thought almost made him laugh aloud given what he had been reduced to, but the longer he listened to the barbarian's repeated chants, and the more time that passed without the man raising a weapon against him, the more he came to realize it was true.

He was unsure how exactly to handle this situation. How does one act a god when one is most assuredly not? The Minotaur had no idea, and he feared what might happen should this man, and some of the others who slept beyond the cave, who he had assumed were guarding against him coming forth, determined he was not in any way holy and divine. The wrath of the pious scorned was legendary throughout history, and he had no desire to be on the end of their swords. At the same time he could not hide from these men, nor did he have any wish to flee and start somewhere again when he had established a life for himself here, meager as it was.

Hardly knowing what he was doing, but realizing still that this very well would determine his path for the coming days and months, the Minotaur walked toward the penitent barbarian. The man ceased his chanting as the Minotaur came to stand over him. The Minotaur could sense the fear that was coursing through the man's veins. He could almost see him cowering on the cavern floor. He stayed standing above him for a long time, as long as he dared, letting the tension blossom into terror. At last, when he felt the man might flee, he leaned down and touched his brow with his hand.

•••

Velthar the Sufferer was the first to be touched by the god and the first to hear it speak, and those two events would set him on his path for the remainder of his days. The god was a beast, alive as any man was, but gods were often that way, inhabiting bodies strange and wondrous and living in the sacred places of the world. His faith, tested the night he had spent alone with the creature in the cavern, never shrinking, even as the terrifying beast had loomed over him, had been proven every day since then in any way Velthar could think. He had brought the god the offerings left by others and had passed along their prayers and words so that the god might hear directly what those outside the cave believed.

The beast had been seemingly oblivious to his obeisances, even as Velthar had begun to tell him of his life, seeking to explain how he had come to be here and what had led him to go before the god in the cave that night. Such a thing was hard to put into words, and he tried day after day to explain himself better, asking the god to guide him further, to tell him what he needed of his servant now that he had been chosen. For months there was no answer, but though the Minotaur showed no outward sign of paying any mind to his words that he could discern in the darkness of the cave, he persisted, feeling that the god approved of what he was doing.

Each evening, as he prepared to leave the cave for his bed beyond its mouth, solitary under the sky, he asked again of the god that had brought him to this place and into the lives of his people and what they were to do for him. One night as he turned to crawl out the entrance, he received an answer, spoken in a halting voice, as though the god were unused to words, and in a strange accent: "You are here to be my eyes."

The voice of the god, so gruff and deep, as huge as the beast itself, nearly sent Velthar into one of his fits. When he had regained his wits he bowed deeply to the god and said, "Why should you, a god, have need of my eyes?"

"Let us go into the light," the god said and they went, Velthar going first.

He turned to face the beast and trembled at the sight of his massive form cast in the shadows of the cave and the sun's final light as it descended behind them. His horns had a greater span than a man's arms and his fists were as large as Velthar's head. It was what remained of the beast's eyes that drew his gaze at last and took his breath away. All that remained of them were whitened scars.

"How is this so?" he whispered.

The Minotaur smiled grimly and Velthar shuddered to witness the depths of his bitterness, the hatred of a god. As with so many of the gods, and all people, he suffered, driven to ends not of his, but fate's choosing.

"It was done so that I could see."

"Yes," Velthar said, belief coursing through him

43

absolute and pure. Here, then, was what had brought the god. He had been blinded so that he could be gifted with the true sight that would allow him to peer into the mists of existence. The beast was to be the oracle of his chosen people and he, the Sufferer, would be his disciple and keeper. His whole body was overwhelmed with electricity at this revelation and he feared he would faint away at the pinnacle of his ecstasy.

"I shall be your guide," he said at last, his voice breaking with emotion.

The god nodded his head severely and then said, in a voice that sounded like boulders being crushed together, "And I shall be yours."

"Where have you come from?" Velthar asked next, and regretted it immediately. The Minotaur's proud face became dark, and for a moment he thought the beast would strike him.

"I was born of a god and a woman in Rheadd, where I lived among the men there. I was one of them, until my father had need and willed that my eyes be taken from me and sent me to live among you."

Velthar shuddered to hear the emotion in the god's voice as he spoke of his past. How he had suffered! He felt a deep kinship with him, though he was but a feeble, broken man. The god appeared lost in contemplation, and Velthar wondered if he had erred in asking of his provenance, if now he would turn to some other of his followers, all gathered just beyond their sight now. The beast seemed to sense his discomfort and he stepped towards him and put one of his mighty arms upon his shoulder.

"I am joyful to be among you now," he said, and Velthar smiled, though a thought twinged in his mind at the way the beast had said those words. Could a god lie?

That was all Velthar had the courage to say to the god that first night now that he had chosen to bless him with his voice, though his soul was afire at the thought of what was to come. He dreamed that night of a temple at the heart of Alari, where the king of his people ruled, and within that temple were he and the beast god and together they ruled the spirit lives of the people as the king ruled the their blood and bone. Such dreams were not unusual for him – he had always suffered so from omens and other torments – so he recognized this sign for what it was.

The next day he told the god of his dream and what it meant. The beast studied him in silence with his dead eyes, which Velthar knew could pierce deeper than any seeing orbs. At last the Minotaur spoke: "These are the concerns of the living. Once, I was one of you, but no more."

Velthar the Sufferer understood what the god was saying. It would fall to him to see this prophecy come to truth. He swore to himself that he would not rest until it was so. That day he went to all the penitents gathered outside the cave, perhaps a half-dozen men, and told them that the god had spoken to him. They all murmured, some in awe, others in consternation, but he held up his hands.

"The god's eyes have been taken from him so that he may see. Ask of him what you will."

One after another the penitents entered the cave, crawling forward on their hands and knees, and asked their question. The god's replies were vague and inscrutable, as gods often were, and several of the men left the cave weeping, so overwhelmed by being in the beast's presence. Velthar took each of them into his arms and then told them to share what they had experienced that day with all they encountered, that the entire world must know of the god and the wisdom he had brought them.

The men left the following day, and when others came in the days that followed, Velthar brought them before the god and then sent them away to tell of what they had seen. Many others undertook the journey to the cave in the following weeks, to ask of the beast what they would of the future or the nature of their lives. Some were fellow penitents like Velthar, who stayed and prayed in the forest surrounding the cave, while others were common folk who desired only to know what the god might tell them. His answers satisfied and word spread further still, and by the next winter the Minotaur had gained the reputation as a great seer, one who should be consulted on all matters of consequence.

In the way of such things, the Minotaur's fame grew, until word of his power came to Alari, where Thedeo ruled, the greatest of the barbarian kings of those parts. Thedeo was intrigued by what he heard of the new god who could see where others could not, and he endeavored to see the beast for himself. The king was deeply troubled by his wife, who could not get with child. His dreams had been filled with fields of vines, heavy with grapes, which, once harvested, shriveled and turned to nothing. Several of his advisors had interpreted the dream to mean that his seed was barren and his wife would never conceive. Ever since then he had dreamed of nothing else, until he had been unable to sleep for fear of watching the fruit shrivel to ashes again.

Thedeo came with a retinue that covered the hills and forest around the cave. He brought with him offerings of gold and silver, the finest of spices and sweetest of perfumes and oils from realms far to the south. These he had his servants bring to the mouth of the cave and set before Velthar the Sufferer, who welcomed the king with the deepest of bows. Rising to his feet, he gestured for him to enter the cave, telling him that he must go alone. Thedeo went, crawling into the darkness as all the penitents did, and soon he was within the cavern and could feel the presence of the god. There he told him of his troubles with his wife and his dreams and the interpretation of his wisest advisors.

The god was seemingly oblivious to his presence, neither stirring at his arrival nor at his speech, and when Thedeo finished the god made no acknowledgment. The barbarian king waited on the ground, his knees sore, and still the beast said nothing. Thedeo began to wonder if he was to receive a response or if he should just go on his way.

When the Minotaur spoke at last it was as if he were a great distance away, deep within the cavern. "Do not let the fruit grow too ripe on the vine."

He would say no more, and Thedeo withdrew and returned home with his advisors, all of whom mulled the god's phrase, wondering at what it meant. It was only once they had returned to Alari that they understood what the god had meant, for in their absence a revolt had stirred up amongst the peasants of the land. The crops, which had been plentiful, were left to rot as they marauded through the countryside, bringing famine to Alari and all the towns of the realm. The onset of winter and the famine allowed Thedeo to bring the rebels to heel. After he had scattered their forces to the wind, he and his advisors realized that the god had been correct. Had he attended to his lands rather than to his own petty concerns about siring an heir, the rebellion would never have come to fruition and the land would have been spared the blight that had befallen it.

The next spring, Thedeo returned to the cave to see the god and prostrated himself before the impassive beast. He thanked the god for his wisdom: "Had I but seen it, I would have saved myself and my people much misery and death."

The god offered no reply, nor even an indication that he had heard. Thedeo hesitated a moment, wondering if he should test the wrath of the beast. After several heartbeats, which seemed to him to echo throughout the cavern, he summoned his courage.

"It would do me and my people an incalculable honor if you would return with me to Alari, the finest city in the land, to be our seer, just as the sibyl is on Hizen."

The Minotaur turned to Thedeo and said, with what the king could almost imagine was a smile, "I thank you for your generosity, but I am not of this world."

"You will not reconsider? Our people have a great need for guidance from one such as you."

"I am here to serve all men. If your people will grant me a place in your city then I will come and all may call on me wherever they come from."

"We shall build you a temple," Thedeo said, forgetting himself in his excitement and rising to look at the beast. The god did not say any more, and Thedeo retreated from the cave to find Velthar the Sufferer.

"The god has agreed to bless Alari if we build him a temple," Thedeo said to him.

Velthar bowed and smiled as though he had expected the king to say exactly that. "I shall see to his journey when the temple is ready."

Thedeo nodded and thanked the penitent. He left for Alari, his heart as light as it had been in years.

•••

Word was sent two years later that the temple had been built and the Minotaur set out for Alari, guided by Velthar the Sufferer and a few of his chosen penitents. His renown had only grown in the past years as word had spread that Thedeo, the greatest of the barbarian kings, was constructing a temple for him. Entire villages turned out to watch the god and his disciples pass by. Those they encountered on the highway, even armies on the march, halted and stepped aside to allow his passage. There were chants and songs and offerings made, and each night the lords of whatever town they happened to find themselves in would squabble over who was to host the caravan of the god.

In each town dozens of seekers would approach the penitents, asking for a moment with the god to share their dreams or ask what their future held. The Minotaur would see them all, answering in his vague and inscrutable way. The supplicants would leave, some weeping, others ecstatic, all overwhelmed by the experience. Many would join the penitents in song and prayer or silent vigil outside the estate where the god was staying, some even asking to join the beast on his journey to Alari.

Among those who asked to join the penitents in service to the god was a young woman named Galrice. She was the daughter of an important local merchant in the town the caravan had come to, known throughout the area, much to the chagrin of her father, for her habit of speaking in foreign tongues. When her father had attempted to marry her to a cousin from another town, with an eye on having this man take over his enterprises, she had refused, saying she had been chosen to serve a god and resisting all attempts to force her to accept the will of her family. That the Minotaur should arrive in their midst not long after only served to settle in Galrice's mind the rightness of her belief.

When she approached Velthar, asking to join with him in service to the god, he refused her, saying that it was not a woman's place, for they were corrupt vessels and the god required purity.

"I have the same faith you do," she told him in reply. "Should not the god decide if I am worthy?"

Velthar conceded that this was proper, and when the Minotaur was finished with the supplicants he stepped within the covered sedan chair that Thedeo had provided for the god's journey. The Minotaur did not need to ask who had come before him; he recognized the scent of the first of his faithful by now.

"There is a woman who wishes to join us on our journey," Velthar said. "She wishes to speak with you of it."

The fire of the Sufferer's belief had frightened the Minotaur at first, and still disturbed him at times, but it had been useful in convincing others. The other penitents who had joined them on this journey all deferred to him as the first to be touched by the god, and he had proved himself not without cunning and skill at organizing this enterprise. Should he ever come to doubt the god, he would be extremely dangerous. For now, his heart allowed no dissent.

"And this disturbs you," he said to his disciple at last.

"It troubles me," Velthar said carefully.

"The penitents of Hizen are both men and women, and I am no greater a power than their sibyls. Do you know of their ways?"

"It is said that the men and women join together in union to better serve the sibyl."

"I am no greater a seer than they. To say otherwise is blasphemy."

"Yes," Velthar said, though there was doubt in his voice. When the Minotaur did not offer anything further, Velthar bowed and said, "I shall bring her to you so that she may be touched by the god."

When the woman appeared at the manor gate that night, she was ushered to the wing the lord had set aside for his honored guest. Velthar waited outside the god's door, and when she bowed before him and had kissed his feet he knocked and ushered her into the darkness within. She stepped forward carefully, unsure of her footing, as the door shut behind her. The beast's presence was marked by his breathing and the stench of animal that clung to him. She moved toward him, stopping when she felt certain that she was near enough for him to touch her.

"I have come before you to ask for the honor of serving you as a penitent," she said, her voice and her legs trembling. She bowed deeply before him, her head pressed against the floor and her eyes closed.

"Why do you ask for such a reward?"

"I have dreamed it."

"Many have dreams."

"Not such as I have," she said, and when he did not respond: "I have dreamed of serving you in the temple in Alari. I dreamed of this day before it came. The words that the Sufferer spoke to me I dreamed and he spoke them as

I had envisioned. And I dreamed that I would receive the touch of the god."

When he said nothing in reply she stood and removed her dress, setting it aside, and awaited the god's touch. As she did so, she thought she heard the god move or cough as if in surprise. After a moment, in which she trembled and thought she would go faint, the god moved, standing from the couch where he had lain, his presence now looming above her. Her teeth chattered and she closed her eyes as she chanted an invocation to the beast. For a long time he seemed not to move, standing close enough that she felt his breath upon her hair and then, at last, the god touched her.

•••

The dreams began after the Minotaur had entered the temple King Thedeo had constructed for him. The temple was a spire lancing towards the sun, with a sole winding staircase spiraling up its center, reaching its pinnacle in a circular room open to the sun. As the Minotaur had been obscured by shadows and darkness in the cave, now he was concealed by the sun, which blinded all who approached him from below. Below the spire's peak were his quarters, which none were allowed to enter, and below that the rooms of his most trusted penitents, Velthar the Sufferer and the woman Galrice. Each was charged with governing the penitents of their sex, as well as the general administration of the temple, such as managing the endless stream of supplicants who came before the god and the offerings they brought. Below their quarters were the offering rooms, where the gifts were kept and where rituals were carried out, and beneath that, at the tower's broad base, were the dormitories where the other penitents slept, as well as rooms of worship.

The Minotaur rarely left the tower or his quarters, and then only to go below to speak with Velthar or Galrice. He preferred to maintain a careful distance with the growing number of penitents, worrying that the reality of his flesh and his other non-godly attributes would lessen their devotion. He still did not understand that among the barbarians these were merely aspects of any deity, for their gods often came among them as men, with the same inherent weaknesses. That he was both wondrous and profane was proof of his godhood, more so than any miracles he might perform.

He had dreamed before, of course, the usual sorts of dreams that all people had. Most he forgot before he even woke, and those that he could recall were mere fragments that amounted to little, with hardly any sense to them. They were nothing like the dreams those who came for his prophecies told him of, which he often wondered at, for he had never experienced anything like a fully formed thought in his sleep. He had assumed that these people had constructed these dreams more fully, whether consciously or not, after waking as they tried to make their sense of the random images sleep brought them.

After he had been blinded he had suffered nightmares, reliving again and again the day of his betrayal. Later in the cave, his dreams had been of his days in Colosi in the pantheon or at various revels. But here in the temple he dreamed no more of Colosi or Rheadd. Instead his dreams were filled with places he had not been and people he had not seen. From what Galrice had told him of Alari and the river valley below the city, it was this place that his dreams set him as witness. He saw the entire city, as though he were able to look down from his perch atop the temple at all the people going about the quotidian tasks of their days. Even Thedeo and his lords and advisors were visible to him within their palace as they conducted the tedious rituals of court, held audiences and conspired.

He saw them all, and recognized them somehow, though he had no way of knowing what they looked like and had only spoken to some of them. Strangely, he could not hear any of them speak. The whole city was silent when he witnessed it in his dreams – even the birds were without song. It was as though in his visions the sense that had been taken from him was returned, but only at the cost of the other that he now relied on. Though it all seemed so real, as though he actually had some means, through augury or otherwise, to secretly visit the lives of others, he gave what he saw little credence, except to wonder why his mind should be calling forth such workaday images and why he should be totally absent from them.

The dreams troubled him little, except for some mild worry as to why they should be so unceasing, night after night, as though he were living the city's day in his sleep. Mostly they were forgotten in the tasks of his day, a tiresome drudgery that he grew to loathe, yet saw no escape from. Supplicants arrived from all corners of the barbarian lands to tell him their visions or the trials set before them and ask for the guidance of a god. He said less and less to them, often only a phrase or two, quoting what the gods had spoken to the great emperors of Colosi from the histories he had memorized in his childhood in Guthril. Often those who came before him were so overwhelmed with emotion, weeping and gnashing their teeth and trembling as though possessed by some demon or spirit, that he doubted they could hear or recall a word of what he said. Yet when they left they thanked him abjectly, with a need in their voices that frightened him.

Worse in their way were the penitents who came to join the worship at the temple under Velthar and Galrice. They were brought to him by one or the other, depending on their sex, and he was expected to test their belief, relenting only at the last moment and touching them so that they were joined to him. This often happened as the sun was setting so that the dying rays framed his massive body as they looked upon him from where they crouched in obeisance. They would chant or pray in the way of the barbarians and he would ask what had brought them before the god. Often it was said that he had spoken to them in their dreams, commanded them to come before them. Always he would say that he had, that there were important tasks for them, and then he touched them with a hand upon their head.

That moment always thrilled him, in a way that nothing had since his battles in the pantheon. For in that moment, as the penitent trembled, or fainted straight away at the mere touch of his hand, he felt something of the power that had been taken from him when he had been blinded. He could, he knew, command these people to do anything, set them to any task his heart desired, and they would do so unquestioningly. It was intoxicating and yet he asked nothing of them, leaving that to Galrice and Velthar, who each came to him to tell him of what they had done and to ask for guidance, which he sometimes gave and sometimes did not. It was enough to know that he could.

Galrice continued to visit his chambers each night, where she would repeat the ritual she had established in their first encounter, chanting an invocation and then disrobing and offering herself to the god to be touched. He would mount her, the frenzy of his lust mirroring that of the penitents who went into fits at the brush of his hand, while she was as unmoved as he in their presence. Nothing he did seemed to stir any emotion in her, yet she accepted it all, and when he questioned her, as he often did in the regretful aftermath of their ritual, she would simply say that he had chosen her.

"What did I choose you for?" he would say. It had begun as a question, but in the intervening months it had become more of a command.

"You have chosen me for union with the god. I dreamed it and it has come to pass."

He would lay a hand upon her head after she said it, blessing her, and she would leave him to spend his night alone. They both might say otherwise, but the Minotaur knew that Velthar the Sufferer and Galrice the Chosen had in fact chose him. And though they might not realize it, it was they who led this temple and the faith they professed, no matter the power bestowed upon him as oracle and guide to all men. He, entrapped by his godhood, could only hope the path they chose was true.

•••

Velthar the Sufferer had grown uneasy in the months since they had entered the temple, ensconcing the god in his chosen place. All had come as his dreams had foretold, and much to his satisfaction he had been given the greatest part to play in seeing it done, and yet his disquiet only grew. The dreams and visions that had so troubled him throughout his life had ceased, the future now a depthless and unending sea through which he must somehow swim. At first it had not concerned him – the god, after all, was now the greatest seer in the land, and he was no longer Velthar the Sufferer but Velthar the First, the one the god had chosen above all others.

But the arrival of Galrice, followed by the god's choosing of her and their union, had troubled him deeply. He had pushed it aside, sensing that it was simple jealously, unbefitting of the First. It was for the god to choose, he knew, and there would others after he had passed from this realm and the god too had taken a new form. These were transient concerns that he had to subsume with his faith and transcend, for he was insignificant and unimportant. They all were before the gods. He had to accept his place before them and find happiness in the role that the god had chosen for him.

That would have been easier had he not lost the visions that, though they had terrified him deeply, had provided a strange comfort and a source of stability in a world that offered few. They had been the constant through all the trials he had endured in his youth, when even his own family had kept distant from him out of fear for what he might be. Still, as he settled into the comforting routines of worship, along with his duties administering the life of the temple and ensuring the harmony of the god, he began to worry that the loss of the dreams signaled some deeper, more troubling change within him. Had he lost his faith?

Faith had been the constant, the driving force in his visions, and when the god had come to them he had given himself freely and fully. He did not doubt the god, for he saw his power demonstrated each day when the supplicants came before him or when a penitent was embraced into the family of the temple. He saw it reflected in the faces of the penitents who joined him in prayer and song beneath the god. He saw it in the faces of the women Galrice chose for union with him under the law of the god. And yet...

The future was closed to him. Why had the god denied him this? Had he wronged him in some way? He knew he had not. It was merely the way of such things. Prophets often had their flame burn out when the time for augury was gone; perhaps it was so with him. He had much to be glad for, and yet a sadness clung to him through what should have been the most glorious days of his life. The days were magnificent but they passed much the same, one into another, unending, and when they were gone it seemed nothing remained.

One evening, in the midst of this melancholy, as he retreated down the steps from the god's chamber, the setting sun still warm upon his back, he met Galrice on her way up. They rarely spoke, except in those rituals that had evolved and which included them both – the morning prayers and the union of the penitents. Galrice smiled, as she always did when their paths crossed.

"You seem weary this evening, Sufferer," she said to him.

He touched a hand to his forehead. "I no longer suffer."

"A blessing of the god, no doubt."

"Perhaps," he said.

"How could it not be, Velthar? We two have been blessed so much, and there are more blessings to come."

"I wonder what shall come now that we have been given so much," he said, almost sighing.

"I have seen it," she said in that fierce way of hers that struck like a blow. "We shall be blessed beyond all imagining."

She did not say more, continuing up the stairs for her union with the god, and he watched her go, wondering what she had seen.

•••

After the arrival of the god to the temple that had been constructed for him, Thedeo had been untroubled by dreams or the anguish that had so regularly haunted his days from the moment he had ascended to the throne as a child following the death of his regent mother, poisoned by some of the local grandees. His father had died earlier from a wound turned gangrenous, and so for most of his unhappy life Thedeo had been surrounded but alone. His advisors and wife, both selected from among the families of those who had poisoned his mother, he could not bring himself to trust, especially after the revolt that he blamed for their misinterpretation of his dreams.

The god he trusted absolutely, and he began to have audiences with him daily, where he would tell of whatever dream had come to him the night before or talk of the problems of the state. Often the god said nothing in response, or only a mere phrase that seemed obliquely related to what Thedeo had said. It mattered not, for there was a comfort for the barbarian king in being in the presence of a seer and a god. Most importantly, he knew he could trust him, for the god owed nothing to the grandees or to Thedeo himself.

It was always late in the day when he left his palace for his audience with the god. He preferred to go as the sun was setting, when all the other supplicants had been received or sent away. The penitents on duty at the temple's doors welcomed him, taking his sword and anointing him with perfumes and blessings. From there he climbed up the winding staircase until he reached the chambers beneath the god's tower, where he was greeted by one of the chosen. He preferred the woman, who always smiled warmly and asked after his family, but today he saw the Sufferer before him.

The man did not acknowledge him, going through the rituals as though he were any other supplicant. Thedeo disliked him intensely for his lack of obeisance before a king. The man was his subject, after all, whatever his service to the god. The Sufferer seemed not to feel that way, though, acting as though he were Thedeo's better. No matter that his exalted position had been paid for with the king's treasure. He would be just another villager passing his days in obscurity were it not for Thedeo and the god. The king voiced none of these thoughts, joining the Sufferer in his invocations and songs and then receiving a blessing for his offering.

This done, he rose and climbed the broad stairs that led to the open tower where the god sat before the day's last light. Thedeo approached on his knees, as he had in the cave, the sun sharp in his eyes, and when he was near enough that he could hear the beast's breathing, he spoke.

On this occasion he had momentous news: his wife was with child. "I must know," he said to the god, "will I have a son to inherit this kingdom?"

He could feel the beast's gaze upon him, though he knew that was impossible in the strictest sense. The god seemed to loom over him, enclosing him, as though into an embrace, though the beast had not moved. Thedeo felt at peace in these moments, awaiting the word of the god. He trusted it, more than his own senses and judgment, and when it came at last, whether for good or ill, he would commit himself to what was said totally.

At last the god spoke: "Want carries the seeds of its

doom. It is a vine that overgrows the heart."

Thedeo felt a chill cut through him at those words. Though he had many questions about what the god had said, he merely swallowed – not without difficulty, for his mouth had gone dry – and went on his way. Who knew what else the god might say? He feared he might be even more terrible. The beast's words to him that night stalked him in the following months, haunting his thoughts whenever he was alone, allowing him no respite. He had two of his wife's ladies stay with her at all times, and had them report to him on her welfare twice a day. The pregnancy went well, and when it came to term a son was born.

All Alari celebrated the news, and Thedeo wept with relief that both mother and child were healthy. The happiness that such a blessing brought him left him uneasy, though, for the god's words were still in his head. What doom awaited him, he wondered – what heartache remained to come? He could not imagine it, and yet it came to preoccupy all his thoughts. Each decision he made was with the god's words in mind, to vanquish whatever evil might be visited upon his family.

Though he tried to speak with the god of those words uttered that fateful day, questioning him on the matter many times when he came before him, the beast was silent on the matter, refusing to say any more. At first he had repeated what he had said that day, as though the explanation was secreted within the phrase itself, but then as the weeks went on and Thedeo became ever more desperate to unlock their meaning, he refused to say anything at all. The silence offered its own danger, for Thedeo knew that he dared not anger the god, or risk being cast into the world unsighted and alone, yet he so desperately needed to know.

Away from the god Thedeo raged against the beast, cursing him until he wept with anguish. What had he done to forsake the god that he would deny him this help in his time of greatest need? Always, though, he would relent and tell himself that, as with his first prophecy, the answer was there for him to find if only fate allowed it. Fate favored the bold, those able to pierce the veil of darkness that shadowed all their lives and strike at that which threatened. It was left to him, then, to find his way through and ensure that when the gods gave him his chance he would be ready to seize it.

•••

The dreams that haunted the Minotaur's sleep were, he had become convinced, not dreams at all but visions of the days to come. It was the barbarian king Thedeo who allowed him to discover the true nature of the dreams. For a very long time he had refused to countenance any thought that these strange night reveries were anything more than evidence of some strange inner compulsion that now haunted him in his blinded state. The apparent reality, the vivid detail of people and places he had never seen, he had dismissed as the fevered overworking of a broken mind. Perhaps it was that, but it was more as well.

Thedeo had continued his daily visits to the god's temple and, after the birth of his son, had become even more unrelenting in his desire to know what the future held for him. He talked endlessly of the grandees and other nobility at court, whom he suspected of conspiring against him, trying to see what the Minotaur would say about each one. The Minotaur kept his counsel as best he could, speaking vaguely and paradoxically as always. However, the true nature of the visions became evident when Thedeo told him of his suspicions about one of his advisors, Athanari, whose family was rumored to have been involved in his mother's poisoning.

One incident the king related to the god in particular seemed taken directly from the Minotaur's dream of the previous night: Thedeo had caught Athanari whispering outside of court with another noble, a man he considered a friend. They had looked so guilty when he had happened upon them that Thedeo confessed he had lost his counsel and yelled at them both, accusing them and their families of grave misdeeds against the kingdom. The Minotaur had in fact seen a scene very similar to that, and what had followed, once Thedeo had calmed himself and apologized to both men, was that the two men had continued with their talk, Athanari gesturing vehemently to where the king had just exited. There had been some more argument and then a consensus had been reached and they had parted with a clasping of their wrists.

The Minotaur said nothing of this to the king, deciding to see what he might learn and use to his advantage with this new ability. In the end it was little, for his dreams were filled with the quotidian stuff of life, rather than the moments of great import that chronicles always reported augers as being witness to. Weeks might pass where nothing of significance occurred, and when something of consequence did take place there was little he could do, the events having determined their course by the time he next spoke to the king.

It seemed to him that the gods were mocking him with this gift, which more and more appeared a sort of curse. He had just enough divination to tantalize, not enough to actually use the power he claimed for himself. This did not surprise him, for the gods were well known for condemning those who pretended to their throne as he now was forced to. To continue to do so could only end in his doom, he knew, and yet he was helpless to stop now that he was entrapped in this temple and lies built within its foundation.

He longed to flee, but he had no idea where to go once he had escaped Alari. His renown throughout this land was such that he could not simply disappear into the countryside. Men and women came from all the nearby lands to witness his godhead. There had even been a few supplicants from Rheadd. Those had been a bittersweet moments, to again be worshiped by his people. In the end it only reminded him of his exile, just as his visions only served to remind him of the dark prison in which he now existed.

The only place in Alari that his visions were blind to was the temple itself, the gods' cruelest irony. For here, where all those who followed him claimed his power as absolute, he had none, a fact made evident when Galrice came to him with word that she was with child.

"It has come as I dreamed it," she said, rising to her feet after he had blessed her following their union.

He waited, not replying, and then she said, her voice trembling, "A godchild grows within me."

"A blessing for us all," he told her at last, glad for the darkness in which they were shrouded, for he did not trust his face in that moment.

"I shall tell the penitents tomorrow. We shall all join to see to the care of this child."

"You honor me."

That Galrice was with child should not have been surprising, given the nature of what they did each night, yet the Minotaur was still shocked at the news. It frightened him as well, for he was unsure how the barbarians would react when one of their own was impregnated by a god. Such stories were often told and written of – certainly the chronicles in Rheadd were filled with such tales – but there was a world of difference between a story told and this. He had no idea how they would react. Would he cease to be a god and become a mere beast, the deity inhabiting his flesh abandoning its earthly bounds? And what then?

His dreams that night were filled with blood. He saw Thedeo gather his most trusted soldiers to him, and at first light send them out to the homes of all the nobles, grandees and courtiers in Alari. They were dragged before the court while their estates were ransacked. One by one they were brought before the king, who condemned them all. Some men were executed, their heads taken to be displayed on the city walls, while others were tonsured and sent with their families into exile. The Minotaur hardly recognized Thedeo as he raged before the humbled grandees, spitting and crimson-faced. He seemed utterly changed from the man who abased himself before the god.

As soon as the Minotaur awoke the next morning he went to the tower above, ignoring the food that the Sufferer had laid out for him. There, if the vision had become reality, he knew he would hear the sounds of anguish in the city below. He stood and listened for a long while but heard nothing, no cries, and no sounds of looting or violence, just the city at the beginning of the day. Relieved, he returned below to his chamber and saw to his duties, expecting to see Thedeo that evening, where he might somehow turn this red tide. But that day the barbarian king did not come to the temple.

The Minotaur was so overwhelmed by his visions and the absence of Thedeo and what might even now be occurring in the city that when Galrice came before him as always he stood apart from her until she fell to her knees, weeping.

"Have I displeased the god?" she said once she had regained herself.

"You are a blessing and a light to me," he said. "Have you not dreamed of what you carry? Do you now doubt it?"

"Never," she said.

He considered her for a moment, listening to their breathing, which sounded in unison. "These are troubled times before us, and my gift demands much of me now."

He stepped toward her and she rose to her feet expectantly. He seized her by shoulders, his fingers pressing insistently into her flesh so that she gasped in pain. "Are you prepared to abandon this place and flee to where the wind takes you?"

"Does my presence anger the god?"

"No," he said. "You shall light the way for me as always. Be ready, for there are dark days before us."

He waited until he felt her nod and then kissed her upon her hair, drinking in the scent that was there. He held her there a moment longer, even as she continued to weep, and then released her. She left him to the darkness and the vision that was to come.

•••

Velthar the First felt shunted aside and ignored in his own temple, the coming godchild now at the center of all their lives. It was a blessing for them all, as he never failed to say to all the other penitents with a wary smile. Yet he could not put aside these black and swelling feelings, try as he might to ignore them. The god had abandoned him, leaving him to darkness and empty dreams, choosing another, first with that woman and now with her child. It was infuriating, though Velthar would not admit that even to himself. It was his dream that had foretold the temple and his efforts that had ensured that it was built. Now he was to be set aside.

He had not been able to summon the courage to voice these thoughts to the god – probably for better given the distracted state the beast had been in these last days. The day after Galrice had announced to the temple that she carried the god's child, Velthar had gone before the god and thanked him for the blessing they had been given, though the words tasted like ash in his mouth.

"A blessing for us all," the god had said in reply.

"We shall all see to the care of the godchild."

The god had considered this for a moment and then had spoken again. "You, Sufferer – you I want to take particular care of the godchild. We shall have great need in the days to come."

Velthar had thanked the god for his kindness, even as he wondered why the beast tortured him so. Not only must he find a way to live with his being forsaken by the god, now he must see to the care of those the god had chosen in his stead. It was a test of his faith, he told himself, but it did not feel so. It felt like an end.

These were uneasy days for everyone in the temple and Alari itself. Following the revelation of the coming of the godchild, Thedeo had struck against those conspiring against his rule. Initially he had arrested a few of the most important grandees, accusing them of all sorts of misdeeds. But after their punishment, when the city had relaxed into its normal rhythms, he had sent his forces out again, seizing other nobles and courtiers, even some merchants, saying that these men too were conspiring against him.

This became the routine of Alari for some weeks: a purge, followed by a watchful period of quiet, only to be succeeded by further arrests and punishment. There seemed no end in sight to the conspiracies that the king uncovered and, in response, many of the remaining important families who had escaped suspicion fled the city, going into exile before the king could send them there. This only served to enrage Thedeo further, and he sent his army, filled with men he trusted absolutely, taken from the lesser families and commoners, to lock the gates of the city, allowing no escape for his enemies.

The populace, unsure of what was to befall them and fearing the king's army, who had taken to ransacking the estates of those who had already received punishment, and a few who had not, stayed in their homes, venturing out only briefly for sustenance. With no one in the city willing to stray far and the gates closed to outsiders, no supplicants came to see the god, and with no offerings those within the temple began to run out of food.

Velthar went before the god as this happened, telling him that were no supplicants and no offerings. King Thedeo, once the first among the faithful of the city, had not ventured to the temple to see the god since he had begun his purges. Velthar voiced the concern that was foremost in the minds of all the penitents: "What if the king has abandoned your glory?"

"Quiet your fears," the god told him, "he shall return."

Velthar accepted this without question, though he was unable to quiet his own growing misgivings. Before, in such moments of crisis, he would have had his visions and his fits to guide him, but now the days and nights were empty of all but fear and doubt. Rumors began among the penitents, and reached his ears, that Thedeo had lost his faith and that soon the purge would turn its bloody eyes upon the god and those who served him. A few even fled the temple as the state of siege showed no signs of relenting. They were not seen again, and word came that they had been butchered by Thedeo's men for being about on the streets without cause.

Hearing this, Velthar went again trembling before the god to tell him what had occurred and to seek guidance, for soon they would be out of food.

"Have I not told you to put aside all worry?" the god said to him. "Thedeo has always honored us."

"I do not doubt you," Velthar said, frightened beyond belief. "But he does not come before you."

"You would believe what those who have no faith say over what your god says in this matter? He shall return. Have faith."

The last words sounded like a thunderclap in the god's tower, and Velthar practically ran from his presence. Retreating to his chambers, he fell to his knees and wept abjectly. So distraught was he that he nearly collapsed into a fit, but it escaped him, leaving him only with a feeling of bleak emptiness that could never be properly filled. The audience filled him with despair, for at last he saw the truth of what had happened these last weeks. The god had not forsaken him for the godchild and Galrice – he had forsaken the god. He had doubted, had put no faith in his wisdom, and so the god had left him in darkness, blind as he to the world.

How could this have happened, he wondered? He had thought – vainly, he saw now – that his faith had matched and exceeded all the other penitents, even Galrice. Instead his had been an empty belief, as insubstantial as the air. This realization so devastated him that he contemplated throwing himself from the tower as a penance, or leaving as the other faithless penitents had, testing what fate had on offer. But the god's words stayed his hand. Had he not asked him, as the First, to care for the coming godchild? To dedicate himself to it?

That night was supposed to be for his union with Helthe, the penitent Galrice had chosen for him, but when she arrived he fell at her knees, crying out, "You must help me. I have forsaken the god and must give penance."

She was shocked at his words and said nothing as he rose to his feet and handed her a whip with four barbed tails. He removed his robe and tunic and abased himself before her again. There was a long silence before he felt the air move and the snap of the leather against his skin. He gasped in pain and Helthe paused, waiting to see if he would stay her hand further. When he said nothing she continued with her ministrations, the barbs tearing at the flesh of his back until he could feel the blood running freely.

His vision and mind swam with pain until an obliterating darkness took hold. From that stepped the god, serenely leaning down to the prostrate Velthar and offering his hand. He took it and the god embraced him and Velthar wept with ecstasy such as he had never known. The god turned from him then and, reaching back into the darkness that still surrounded them both, brought forth the godchild and handed it to Velthar. The beast bowed in obeisance before the godchild and went back again into the darkness, leaving only the Sufferer and the child.

•••

The Minotaur could sense the fear of those around him at what was occurring in the city at the hand of their benefactor, the mad king Thedeo. That he had gone mad seemed of little doubt now to the Minotaur, given his endless purge and the bottomless suspicion that fed it. Still, he had continued to counsel patience to Velthar and Galrice, hoping that they would do the same with the rest of the penitents. There was little else they could do but wait and hope. The Minotaur knew an opportunity would come to set them all on a better path; his dreams of blood had ended and he saw the day when Thedeo would come before him again.

Each day the barbarian king did not emerge from his palace, though, the Minotaur's doubts grew. The penitents were growing restless, fearful of what might happen to them should the siege continue, and when what little food remained was gone. How long before they turned on the god they worshiped, blaming him for what was befalling them? Worst of all was Velthar. He could no longer trust the man, which saddened him, though he knew he had never been deserving of the faith the Sufferer had invested in him.

From the first moments of the siege Velthar had come to his god with worries of what was to befall them, and the Minotaur had tried to assuage them to no avail. He had persisted, coming to him with each new rumor that reached the temple, asking again and again if Thedeo had forsaken them. Then, just as the Minotaur had begun to prepare for the man to turn against the god, the Sufferer came before him, stinking of blood and in agony, begging for forgiveness for doubting him.

"Thank you for showing me the light and the truth of my failures," Velthar said to him, weeping in a fervent ecstasy as he did so.

The Minotaur was careful not to step away from the penitent, though his revulsion compelled him to. "What have you done?"

"I have given penance for my lack of faith. I had forsaken you in my heart, though I did not know it."

"I am grateful for it."

"The path was the true one, as you foretold," Velthar said. "I have no doubts now. You have shown me and at last I am able to see."

"And what have you seen," the Minotaur said, being careful to keep the question from his voice, issuing it instead as a command.

Velthar began to weep again. "Oh, my god, my god. You have given me the greatest gift and the greatest honor. When you go from this body to that of the godchild, it is I who will be entrusted with your keeping. As you have said to me, and yet I did not believe."

The Minotaur shivered at those words, for the seeds of his own destruction were plain in them. Had he somehow brought this madness on this city, he wondered, before dismissing the thought. He was not a god after all.

"I am glad of it," he said at last. The Sufferer uttered his final blessings and then retreated, still on his hands and knees, chanting his prayers as he went.

That night the Minotaur again dreamed of Thedeo's return to the temple, though his sleep was fitful. When he awoke late in the night, in the midst of one of his visions, he realized he had been crying aloud, saying again and again, "The flower has gone to seed and they must all be rooted out."

He shivered to himself and wondered what he meant by that. It seemed to him though that the price would be terrible.

•••

The visions had not returned to Velthar the Sufferer as he had supposed. Only through the penance he had imposed upon himself, the mortification of his own dear flesh, did the god allow him to see as he had formerly. He was being tested, he understood, for his faith had been proven weak and now he would have to demonstrate the strength of it. He had Helthe come to him each night to minister to him the salvation of the barbed whip. His back was now scored with the wounds, many of which never had the chance to heal over. Though Helthe always applied salves of various sorts that she had procured through some mysterious means, several of the cuts were infected and he now passed his days in the heat of fever.

The vision that changed everything came the day before Thedeo returned to the temple and the grace of the god. Helthe whipped him until he lost control of his senses, and there again was the darkness, which he now embraced, for he knew the light which would follow upon it. This time, though, the darkness did not cease. Instead he heard a sound, the guttural sounds of an animal, and he stood and went toward it. Here there were still shadows but he could see, as though through the dimness of the gloaming. He followed the sound through the nothingness that surrounded him and emerged into the god's chamber.

What he saw there made him fall to his knees in despair at the desecration he witnessed. The god was there, but he was not the god, he crawled about like a mere beast. Galrice was there as well on her hands and knees, and the two of them sniffed at each other as though they were the basest of creatures absent the god's incandescent touch. Velthar could not imagine witnessing anything more horrifying than these unholy actions in the temple of the god, but the worst was still to come. Galrice crawled before the god and knelt down so that her rump was lifted to him. The god mounted her and began to rut, both of them emitting a keening sound Velthar could not understand. When they were through Velthar saw that her belly was full with child and then the darkness became whole again.

When he returned to himself Helthe was at his side, pressing a damp cloth to his face and whispering an invocation to the god. Velthar's jaw ached as though he had been clenching it, and there was a taste of blood in his mouth. For a moment he lay, allowing Helthe to see to his needs, his mind empty of thoughts, but then he recalled what he had just seen and pushed her aside. He rose unsteadily to his feet and went from his chambers across the hall to where Galrice lay, as Helthe watched him, saying nothing.

She was awake still, kneeling in prayer, a sole candle providing light. Her profile was to him, the fullness of her belly evident. Seeing it caused him to retch, which startled her. She had been so deep in her prayer she had not heard his entrance. Now she turned, her face agape at the sight of him. When she saw the expression on his face she shrank away as though she expected some harm to befall her. Velthar followed her eyes and saw that his hands were clenched into fists, and he forced himself to breathe and let his hands free.

"Your trickery is at an end," he said, approaching her.

"What is this madness?"

"Do not play the fool with me," he shouted, spittle flying from his mouth. "I have seen it. You have been sent to ruin us, to lead us down the path of false worship of your demon child."

This sparked Galrice's anger, and she rose to her feet to confront him. "The god himself has claimed the child as his own. How can you deny it? He has entrusted the both of us to its care."

He shook his head, laughing at her. "You are a foul and cunning demon. You nearly ensnared us all. The god set it as a test for me and I nearly failed. But I have overcome my weakness and now he has returned to my heart and shown me the truth."

"Well, let us go before him now and see what he says of the truth you speak."

Velthar agreed and they went up the stairs to the beast's chambers for an audience with the god. Galrice was praying under her breath as they went, and in that moment

Velthar understood that this moment was merely another test. The god had left it to he alone to see that the demon was cast out from their midst. As they came to the god's chambers he seized her by the hair and dragged her up the stairs to the tower above. She struggled fiercely, scratching and clawing in an animal frenzy, screaming all the while.

When they reached the tower he did not hesitate, pulling her to the tower's edge. Here her tactics changed and she ceased her screaming and her struggles and begged him to spare her, to spare the godchild. He listened to none of it and sent her tumbling over the edge. A terrible wail rose up from her as she plummeted to the earth, the demon host leaving her corporeal form. Following that there came a blessed silence and he descended below to tell the god.

●●●

The Minotaur had not yet fallen asleep when the screams reached his ears, startling him from his bed. He stayed rooted to the floor as the cries disappeared above him, visions of Thedeo's army storming the temple and laying it to ruin paralyzing him. He still had not moved when the final scream, louder than all that had come before, sounded. Nor did he in the silence that followed, a quiet that told its own tale. He knew he should be heading below, summoning Velthar and Galrice and attempting to flee, if that were still possible. But he did not, for the greater part of him wanted this charade ended at last, so that he could descend to that greater peace where his sleep would be unmarred and the days endless.

Velthar entered his chamber a moment later, bowing before the god. The Minotaur could smell sweat upon him. "I have done as you asked," he said.

"What is that?" He could not keep the fear from sounding in his voice.

There was a pause and then the Sufferer spoke. "I have done as you showed me in the vision. I have removed the demon host and her spawn."

The Minotaur felt his blood go still. *What have I created? A madman, truly.*

"I shall see to the preparations for the coming of the new god."

All the Minotaur could summon in that moment was, "I am grateful."

It was enough; Velthar left him to his own thoughts, which were few, an absolute emptiness enveloping his being. It was as though his blindness had extended to consume his entire being. He heard nothing, smelled nothing, felt nothing. When he emerged from the spell of his reverie, his heart was so filled with despair he could not even weep, could not rage or curse, could only sit in the terrible silence. This was the moment for flight, he knew. The path to the gates he could recall from his dreams, and he thought himself strong enough still to overpower the guards on watch. And if not, so be it. Better that than to persist amidst such lunacy, all committed in his name.

What stayed his hand was the thought of Velthar sending Galrice over the tower's edge to her death. What had possessed the Sufferer? Had his fits at last overwhelmed his greater faculties? From his thoughts grew a rage, the likes of which he had not felt since the first days of his exile from Rheadd. Those terrible days, when his entire mind had been consumed with what had been done to his women and servants and to him as well. He had been helpless then to stop it, all those who had conspired against him ensuring that. Now, though he was blind, he was not without means. The god could still speak through him, and Thedeo was still to come. He would see to it.

That night he did not sleep, his anger burning like a torch in his soul. He did not leave his chambers the next morning, as he normally did, keeping vigil in Galrice's memory in the Rheadd manner and plotting his next steps. The gods would surely not forgive his inaction now, not after the months he had spent harvesting the sorrow of others with his lies. Late in the day, as he was in the midst of his prayers to the true gods, Velthar arrived to tell him that Thedeo had arrived.

"It was as you prophesied," the Sufferer said, his voice ringing out. The Minotaur resisted the urge to tear him limb from limb, though he sorely wanted to, and instead said nothing. Death was too kind a punishment for the man, he had decided. He would see this whole temple brought to the ground so that all the Sufferer had built would lie in ruin.

He received Thedeo atop the tower, a mist wetting both their brows, the breeze cutting. The barbarian king wept at the sight of the god. From his dreams the Minotaur knew that Thedeo had been changed irrevocably by the purge he had embarked on. He had visited a reign of terror upon his own subjects and his own suspicions had eaten at him until he was but a shadow of his former person. His hair, once a lustrous brown that shone in the glare of the sun, was now white, and his face was nearly as bloodless. He walked differently now, the Minotaur noticed as he approached, sounding like a man who had entered into his last feeble years. He did not doubt that it was so.

"I must thank you, I have no words," Thedeo said to him. "You have guided me through the darkness to the light. I have faced the doom of my own want and cut out the vines of evil that threatened to overwhelm this kingdom."

"I am grateful that I have been a help to you. Your service to me and those here in this temple has not been forgotten."

"I am sorry that I have neglected you," Thedeo said, his voice raw with emotion. "Your chosen has told me it has been a trying time. I can only beg your forgiveness and say that I was only following your warning."

The Minotaur gathered his thoughts before he spoke. The next words would have to carry weight beyond their meaning, he knew. "There is no anger in my heart. You have walked with grace. And you must continue to do so, for the burden is not lifted. The flower has gone to seed and they must all be rooted out."

He heard the breath go from Thedeo with some satisfaction. "How can this be?" he said in disbelief. "I have done—"

"Do not question yourself. Cast your eyes where they have not gazed before. There lies your ruin."

Thedeo seemed taken aback. "It cannot be," he muttered, before remembering himself. "I shall scour my heart. I shall never rest."

The Minotaur resisted a smile until the king had departed. Velthar awaited him below, he knew, for the day was near its end, but he allowed himself a few moments alone. The mist thickened to a rain, leaving him soaked, but still he did not move until he could feel the darkness of the night taking hold around him. Then he rose to his feet and went below to face the Sufferer.

Velthar awaited him outside his chamber door and he was not alone – the Minotaur could smell a woman beside him. He entered his rooms without a word, and after a moment they followed behind him, paying obeisance as they came, their chants forming a strange melody. The Sufferer stank of fresh blood again, the Minotaur noted, his wounds now reopened. His voice, to the Minotaur, had a deranged frenzy to it, a man on the edge of some precipice.

"I have done as you asked," Velthar said to him, "as you showed me in the visions you granted me. I have prepared the way for the arrival of the godchild."

The Minotaur was silent, unsure what Velthar was referring to.

"The false worship of the demon has been overthrown," the Sufferer continued. "The god is for all."

"You speak the truth."

"Thank you for your blessing," Velthar said, and the

woman with him echoed his joyful phrase. "And as the god is for all, union with the god should not be the domain of one, it should be for all of our female penitents. All must share in the duty of raising the godchild, all should have the opportunity to receive the blessing of carrying it."

The Minotaur stayed silent, which the Sufferer took as his assent and proceeded with his ceremony. "The blessed Helthe shall be first," he said, rising to his feet.

The woman began to chant as though possessed by some spirit and then rose to her feet as well. Velthar removed her robes and anointed her body with a sweet-smelling oil. This done, she crouched before the god, offering herself to him. Velthar began to sing one of his prayers, seeking his blessing. The Minotaur did not stir from where he sat, hatred of the Sufferer coursing through his veins. He was to be used as breeding stock for this man's herd, and everything in him revolted at the idea. Only his revenge, which he had set in motion, stilled his heart enough to allow him to act. He rose to his feet and approached the waiting penitent, mounting her. Velthar did not cease his singing until the union was through, and then both he and woman left, their chanting invocations lingering in their absence.

He wept when they had gone, rage and despair filling his soul. He had doomed himself, he knew, with his lies and his acceptance of this false worship. The gods would not forgive him and he accepted that. Galrice had been innocent in this, betrayed only by what she thought her visions were telling her, and his own lies. Her blood was on his hands and he would see that Velthar answered for it, no matter the indignities that he must endure.

The days that followed were agony as he had never known. He was unable to sleep – no matter what draughts he took or how much wine he drank, it eluded him, and he wandered his quarters like a creature who had already died. After being hounded by so many pointless visions, it was a bitter irony that they should be taken from him at the very moment of his need. Thedeo did not return to the temple, though Velthar told him the purges continued, the king turning upon his army and those of his advisors and friends who he had kept closest to him through the last terrible months. It would only be a matter of time, he knew, before he turned on the god he followed, for who could remain?

The moment could not come soon enough, for Velthar had been as good as his word and brought a different penitent before him every night for union. It felt to the Minotaur in those moments as though he were the god and that his spirit was dissipating into each of these women, forming a new god and leaving him a husk of a thing, a mere beast. All as the Sufferer had foreseen.

•••

Mad Thedeo, as he was now known throughout the land, began his final day upon the earth as he had every day since the god had arrived at the temple he had built for him. He stepped out from his chambers onto the dais that overlooked all of Alari from atop the palace's great tower. The temple of the god loomed above him, the shadow it cast at first light falling upon the dais where he now knelt and offered his morning invocations to the beast who could see through the mists of time and existence. As he chanted, his servants anointing him with incense from braziers, he heard the first cries on the streets below. He paid them no mind, finishing his prayers and going within to eat his breakfast.

By the time his meal was done, the sound of the crowds outside had grown to such a volume that he returned to the dais to see what was happening. Looking at the streets below, he could see mob forming at the palace gates. Noticing him above them, the crowd reached a frenzied pitch in their cries, throwing rocks and other projectiles at the guards on duty, demanding that the gates be opened. Thedeo turned to his servants to ask him to summon his remaining counselors, only to hear a roar as the gates swung open.

For a moment he stood disbelieving as the crowd charged into the palace. Some of his own soldiers were among the first to cross the sacred threshold they had sworn to protect, and he saw that the guards were not offering any resistance to the intruders. At last, as the marauders began to ransack the grounds and a few forced their way into the palace tower, he regained his senses and turned to order his servants to gather his jewels and gold, so that they might flee the city. But they were gone and he was alone.

He wandered in a daze through his chamber and beyond, finding the rooms – normally filled with servants, counselors and courtiers all awaiting his appearance – empty. The dim sounds of the mob and its depredations reached his ears, but he paid them no mind. Nor did he go to any of the secret passages, which had been built expressly to allow the king to flee an insurrection.

"How did I fail you?" he said aloud, but no answer was forthcoming.

Thinking then that he should go before the god and ask why he had been forsaken, he started toward the gates. Before long he encountered the mob, but he paid them no mind, wandering through their carnage, thinking only of getting to the god so that he might receive his guidance. For their part, the crowd was startled by his appearance; he looked like a man who had aged twenty years in a day and had a stare so vacant that some whispered his soul had already fled, leaving only his flesh before them. This lasted until one of his soldiers stepped forward and struck Thedeo in the face, knocking him to ground. The mob as a whole followed, swallowing up the king's form, beating him and tearing at his flesh until there was nothing remaining that resembled a man.

After the looters completed their destruction of the

palace, leaving the place in flames with no one remaining to quench the fire, they turned to the temple that their mad king had built for what they now knew to be a false god. They rushed toward the forbidding spire, calling for the beast to be brought before them so that it too could be punished for all they had suffered. As they approached, the doors to the temple were thrown open and the penitents emerged to echo their chants, to the delight of the crowd. The god's followers stepped aside, allowing the mob to enter the main hall where the daily worship was held.

There they saw the god, his arms and legs chained and his back streaked with blood. A woman whipped him to the rhythm of his Chosen's prayers while another penitent wafted incense around them. The beast moaned and shuddered terribly with each blow, its dead eyes streaming with tears. In spite of his fearsome size, the beast seemed unable to rise, and he made no struggle against the chains that bound him. A few in the crowd saw why and began to whisper, for the beast had been lanced with a sword through his ribs. A pool of blood gradually began to spread around the floor where the beast was sprawled.

Velthar the Sufferer finished his prayers and turned to the crowd as the woman ceased her whipping.

"Know that the god is not false," he said, ignoring the angry murmurs that rose among those assembled. "Know that he is true and good. This test of our faith that he has set before us has been heavy indeed, but we have passed it, throwing off the shackles of the mad king so that we may fall under the kingdom of the god."

A tense silence followed, those from Alari glancing at one another, all of them unhappy with what they were hearing but still unable to bring themselves to turn against a god. What if they were proven wrong and this all had been a test of faith, one in which they were found wanting?

"I too, like you, doubted. I lost faith. But the god did not abandon me and he has not abandoned you. Nor has he abandoned this city that has embraced him. Thedeo was a false believer; he sought only to protect his kingdom and his riches. The god has shown us that nothing shall come of such vanity.

"This terrible beast was the mark of our faithlessness. The god has left this form. But he has shown me, he will return again. From the wombs of one of these penitents here a new god shall emerge to rule the new kingdom we have created here this day. I have seen it."

He began to pray, as did the other penitents, their cries rising up from all around the room. Slowly, one by one, those in the mob joined the chants and songs as the woman began to whip the beast again, the rhythm of the blows leading the prayers to a crescendo. With that complete, Velthar raised his hands to quiet the crowd.

"This beast will now be taken from this sacred place, taken from this sacred city and returned to the wilds from whence he came. When that is done the city shall be reborn."

Cheers went up from the assembled. Velthar and the woman released the chains that bound the beast's feet and hands, replacing them with a large collar and chain about his neck. With Velthar pulling at the chain and the woman behind urging him on with her whip, the Minotaur was led through the streets of Alari, leaving a trail of blood in his wake. Too weak to stand, he crawled on his hands and knees like a common animal. The crowd followed behind, cheering each blow that struck from the whip, singing songs of the new days to come.

The gates to the city were opened for the first time in weeks as the procession reached the city wall and the Minotaur was led out. There Velthar released him, taking off the collar and chain. He crawled away, having no sense of where he was going. For a time he seemed to be on a road, but then he left it and the sounds of the crowd and city grew distant and at last disappeared. There he stopped and lay on the cold ground, the sun gone from the sky, and waited for sleep to come.

THREE:

THE WONDROUS BEAST

MONTHS PASSED IN MISERABLE solitude for the Minotaur, where he survived on berries and whatever he could manage to scavenge. He was avoided as a pariah wherever he went in Thedeo's kingdom, for word had passed quickly from Alari of his downfall. No longer a god, but a mere beast, towns barred their gates to him and villagers rang bells to warn others of his approach. Children, tempted by the stories they had heard of his former deity, would follow him at a distance, throwing stones at him for fun.

Though he longed for death, and had expected it after what Velthar had done to him, the gods did not grant him release. His crimes were too great, he surmised. His wounds healed well, though he was left greatly weakened, with little of the strength he had once possessed, and his sides were still marked with scars where the whip had torn at his flesh. His visions had ceased upon leaving Alari, returning him to that darkness again, which he took as a small mercy. He often woke weeping and trembling, his mind empty; whatever dreams that had troubled him vanished into the aether.

In a sense he had died when Velthar and his followers

had cast him from the temple, his false godhood passing from him, for in the long and empty days that came after not once did he think of what was to come. Such things no longer mattered to him. He lived on because he could not summon the courage to stop himself, scrounging and foraging, a pathetic figure on the fringes of the world. He hated himself for this weakness. No flame burned within him to keep on, nothing beckoned him forward, yet on he went, unable to stop himself.

Some days, when he had walked too long and exhaustion had overcome him, he would collapse, wherever he happened to be, and lie there insensible, thinking about Galrice. He would imagine their escape from Alari and their child – a son, he was certain – that they raised to be a proud man. All impossibilities, he knew. Galrice would never have left the temple, perhaps not even at his command. She had believed, they had all believed, and when that belief had proved to be upon a foundation of sand, it could only crumble and ruin them all.

It was while lost in such despairing thoughts as these that he fell into the hands of Doctor Eid and His Traveling Cabinet. The Minotaur had passed beyond Thedeo's kingdom and into another barbarian fiefdom, where the learned doctor happened to be displaying his bestiary. Upon hearing from the locals of a strange half-bull, half-man who had once been a god, he sent two of his minions to capture the beast. It was an easy task, for by this time the Minotaur had fallen into a pitiable state. His ribs showed through his chest, his gums were bleeding and he had a tremor in one leg that made his gait unsteady.

The good Doctor's minions found him lying and daydreaming in the middle of some country trail, muttering to himself in some strange language. They set upon him before he even realized they were present, knocking him senseless with a few sharp blows from a cudgel. They fashioned a length of rope into a halter and put it about his neck, running it through a ring they put through his nose, and with that they led him as they might any draft animal.

The Minotaur offered no struggle in the face of these new humiliations, submitting meekly to the two men as they led him back to the village where Doctor Eid had established himself. He could hear the gathered crowd murmur in consternation as he passed by. For a fleeting moment he thought they might act, turn against his captors and restore his freedom to him, but he quickly realized their anger was directed at him. In the months since his exile from the temple, Velthar had been careful to spread word to all and sundry that not only had the god left the Minotaur, he was now an empty vessel who could be inhabited by any false devil or wizard.

Seeing him in the possession of this foreign doctor who sold various strange life elixirs and talked of the secret knowledge of science and philosophy that he possessed, they suspected the two of them of being in league. By the time the Minotaur had been thrown into a cage and tossed some hay, which he lay down on as a bed, the villagers had begun to gather, even calling the farmers and herders from the fields to stand against this invasion. The good Doctor, seemingly oblivious to the growing ire of the villagers, stepped out before them, and in his best barker's voice began to call for them to come and look upon their fallen god.

"My good friends. Come and see the god that has fallen to earth," he said in his strange accent. "Once a god, now a mere beast. But a singular beast. Part man and part bull. What terrible congress led to such a creation? Only the gods know, and they have sent him from their care so that you may look upon him and the offspring of such a terrible act."

The crowd had begun shouting at him before he had even finished his speech, and several of them took up stones and aimed them at the Minotaur's head.

"My good friends, my good friends. This is not necessary. The beast has been subdued. I have him in my grasp. He shall not escape."

"Yes, he is under your control," one man shouted. "We all know what that means. You'll not be ruling over us."

"My good friends, I have no designs upon your land or your hearts. I would never dare to usurp your gods or your rulers. I am a humble servant and I ask only for some of your time and your hard-earned coin so that you may witness my wondrous menagerie. Creatures, each more marvelous than the next, from all corners of the earth, carefully gathered and tamed and brought before you."

His words did little good, for the crowd had already decided against him, and he was forced to have his men hitch up the caravan and flee before the villagers turned violent. When they were safely underway, he had the driver of his wagon pull alongside the one carrying the Minotaur's cage so that he could study the creature more closely. He clucked his tongue in disapproval at the shriveled and ragged state of the beast, but soon he found himself nodding and smiling.

"Not some simulacrum here. The unvarnished truth lies before us," he said to the driver, who spat in reply.

"You had better be worth the trouble you've caused me," the Doctor called to the beast. "I'll have to leave these miserable lands now or they'll have my head. And think of the coin I am losing because of it. If they believed you a god, they would have believed anything."

The Minotaur had been dozing, but he awoke at the Doctor's words and raised his head, trying to discern the man's tongue. "What words are these? Where are you from?" he said in the barbarian tongue he knew the Doctor spoke.

"It speaks," the Doctor said. "A truly wondrous beast. We hail from the magnificent and eternal empire Huiam, all praise its greatness. You have not seen its like in these miserable barbarian realms."

"I see little as it is," the Minotaur said. "And I am no barbarian. I am a patrician of Rheadd."

"His tales grows even more fantastic. Well, beast, I think we shall find use for you." The Doctor laughed and slapped the driver's shoulder so that he pulled the caravan ahead of the Minotaur's cage, leaving him to shiver and wonder what the man meant.

•••

Once they had passed from those barbarian lands where the Minotaur's renown had reached, he became the star attraction of the *Traveling Cabinet of the Ingenious Doctor Eid, Containing Creatures Both Marvelous and Monstrous.* He was kept chained in the cage, though it was hardly necessary. He had neither the physical strength nor the will to engineer an escape. The days soon all passed in the same manner. The caravan would arrive in a town, criers going up and down the streets, calling on the populace, who would wander in to view the bestiary on display while Doctor Eid spoke to them all of the strange habits and marvelous natures of the creatures within. He would then offer those gathered the life elixirs he had created, drawing them, he said, from the essences of his menagerie, containing some part of their marvelous properties.

"Guaranteed, my good friends, all is guaranteed," he said each time, in the seemingly endless number of tongues he seemed to be familiar with. "This is not mere magic, there is no waving of wands or any such chicanery involved. I am a doctor and a man of science. What I give to you is not just an elixir but the product of centuries of learning and knowledge, passed down in secret by the greatest philosophers of Huiam, and now in my humble possession."

The other creatures in the Doctor's bestiary were mundane, obvious fakes to all but the most credulous. The Minotaur was something else entirely, and people recognized him as such and looked on in wonder and horror. Soon the Kilag Dragon and the Harpy of Nesu, ordinary creatures that had been dressed up to appear fantastic, were all but ignored, the deception all the more obvious in the face of the Minotaur's manifest realness. The Doctor began to drape the Minotaur's cage in black curtains, even as they traveled between towns, to keep the beast hidden from view. He would lead the spectators past the lesser creatures of his bestiary, only revealing the Minotaur at the final moment, ensuring that his appearance was all the more powerful and dramatic.

The reactions of these foreigners – rubes and barbarians all, according to the good Doctor – confirmed his belief that he had inadvertently stumbled upon the very thing that would assure his reputation in Huiam. For years he had wandered far-flung foreign realms, his ambitions to be recognized as a philosopher and scientist in his native land thwarted, forced to survive on mean deception to keep food on his plate. When the Doctor had set out on his self-imposed exile, it had been for the purpose of exploring the far corners of the wondrous earth and returning triumphant with specimens and tales unheard of and unseen by any, just as his heroes had. That he had failed so utterly in achieving this, and been reduced to a mean charlatanry, only whetted his ambitions further and made the discovery of the Minotaur taste all the sweeter.

On their journeys between towns the Doctor would make sure his caravan rode beside the beast's, and he endeavored to teach him the golden tongue of Huiam, so that when the time came for him to return triumphant to the eternal land the creature would be able to perform. The Minotaur was happy for the distraction from his mean existence and was intrigued by what the strange Doctor had to say of the empire and its fabled cities. He doubted much of what the man said, for it was clear to him that he was an inveterate liar, one who had made such a habit of it that the lies had become the truth, even to his own ears. But if even half of what he said of Piufenh, the imperial capital, was true then it was a city to rival Colosi.

"My good friend, you have never seen its like," Doctor

Eid would say to him. "Marvelous architecture. The most ancient of temples, dedicated not to gods but to science and philosophy. The Eternal Palace, where none but the empress and her chosen may enter. And the streets. None of these haphazard constructions that you see in these parts. They are the product of design and thought, broad and wide and laid out on a grid, as sensible as can be.

"I can hardly wait to return to the Academy to show them my discoveries. They sent me off with such fanfare, you know. An exploration of all the world, known and unknown, to match the likes of Goin and Jwuik. And now I shall return with a wonder never before imagined, let alone seen. The empress herself will want to see it."

The Minotaur offered no comment on these matters, especially not the fact that he was the "it" who the empress would want to see. The man seemed oblivious to his true nature, even as he spent day after day painstakingly teaching the Minotaur his language. To the good Doctor he would always be a mere beast, no matter that he had told him of his patrician birth and his triumphs in the pantheon, and a beast must be kept caged and chained. The Minotaur made no complaint on the matter, preferring to bide his time, for the Doctor was feeding him well. He could already feel his strength returning, along with the luster of his coat. In time, when he had proven his intelligence and native reasoning, no doubt the Doctor would see fit to set him free. For even more marvelous than a beast caged was one that walked about as any other man.

Meanwhile, he came to enjoy those moments in the good Doctor's show when the curtain would be pulled aside to reveal his presence. The crowds, ever growing, for word had begun to spread of the fantastic creature that traveled with Doctor Eid, would always let out a gasp somewhere between fright and disbelief at the sight of him. As his strength returned to him, the Minotaur took to standing in his cage when the moment of revelation was about to commence, the better to impress those gathered with his stature. The cage was not quite tall enough to allow him to stand freely, and so he was forced to hunch over, which gave the appearance of him being about to burst free of its confines, titillating the audience further.

The Doctor was delighted at his newfound showmanship and told him that when they came to Huiam they would set him upon a stage and have him retell the sad story of his life in his new tongue. "Imagine when they hear you, speaking as a man, not a barbarian. What they will say. A civilized beast."

•••

The Doctor's caravan traveled on through more and more lands, none of which the Minotaur was familiar with. It seemed every day brought new dialects being spoken and the scent of perfumes and spices unknown to him. It all startled and delighted him, his senses overwhelmed, and his imagination taking flight as his mind sought to color what his ears and nose told him. Who had known that the world was so large? For a time the lands they passed through seemed much the same in their geography as those he was familiar with. Here was a the smell of a forest and there the vast quiet of a plain and now the brisk cool of the mountain air struck his lips.

But after some weeks they came into a desert, a grim and empty place filled with rock and ruin. According to the Doctor the place had once been home to an empire to rival even Huiam, but time and fate had undone that. Once water had flowed in these places, and cities with splendorous gardens had been constructed, but now it was barren, with only a few stunted trees and roads that led to fiercely guarded watering holes. It was a lawless place, ruled by bandit kings, where no one caravan was safe, so the Doctor banded together with some merchants who were bringing spices back to Huiam, hoping the strength in their numbers would keep them all safe.

The Minotaur's caravan was covered throughout the journey, the Doctor hoping to keep his existence a secret from his fellow travelers and any others they encountered. Such a desire was hopeless given the close quarters in which they traveled, both while on the road and camping at night. That the Doctor was perpetually checking in on his precious cargo to ensure that it was secured and safe only further demonstrated to everyone the importance he placed on it. He would often slip away from the nightly gatherings of his fellow Huiamites and attend to the Minotaur, continuing his lessons so that he would be well prepared when they arrived at Piufenh, which only drew more suspicion upon the covered caravan.

Speculation among the other merchants was wild. That there was a beast within was beyond any doubt, for that was the good Doctor's standard ware, and several of them had observed his servants bringing food to the caravan as they did to the others. What was different, they noted to their fellows, was the quality of the food. It was a meal fit for a man, no doubt, which gave them all pause. One of the merchants took it upon himself to steal after Doctor Eid when he left them for the Minotaur's wagon. He watched as one of the Doctor's servants let him into the cage and kept a vigil until his master left. He was certain that he could hear the Doctor and another speaking, sometimes in his native tongue and other times in a strange barbarian dialect.

This revelation led to even greater interest for all concerned, for everyone agreed that whatever kind of beast was in there must be of incalculable value if it could speak as a man. Several of them began to plot to steal whatever magnificent creature was hidden there, thinking their fortunes would be made if they could get it to Huiam, where any number of princes would pay unholy sums to add it to their menageries. Alliances were formed and the opportune moment argued over for when to strike and seize the creature, for everyone knew that their fellow travelers were deep into planning as well.

All their plotting came to nothing, for not a week after the merchant's revelation as to the nature of the beast, the entire caravan was struck by bandits. They attacked at first light as everyone was in the midst of breaking camp with tents being taken down, horses being fed and harnessed and the many of the merchants, including Doctor Eid, in the middle of eating their breakfast. The bandits swept down from the cliffs that stretched out above them, rocky outcroppings that provided ample hiding space for an ambush. The caravans were thrown into utter chaos, the bandits striking down any man they came near and scattering the horses before setting about to collecting their plunder. They took from the wagons whatever could be easily carried on their pack horses: aromatic spices, fabulous clothes and whatever gold and silver the merchants had hidden in their belongings.

When they came to Doctor Eid's bestiary they dispatched most of the creatures without so much as a glance until they came to the shrouded caravan. They tore aside the cloak to see what was within and gasped at the sight of the Minotaur, momentarily unsure of what to do. Doctor Eid, who had hidden himself among the ruins of the camp, chose that moment to show himself, and he fell to his knees, begging the bandits to spare both himself and the magnificent creature within.

"My good friends," he beseeched them, "there is no need to kill us. This magnificent creature is worth far more to you alive than dead."

"That may be," one of them, the leader by all appearances, said. "We have no need of you, though."

"On the contrary, my good friends, on the contrary. The beast can speak. A miracle of miracles. But it is in a tongue unheard by your ears. Only I can make sense of it. So his value is tied to mine, for only I can give him voice."

"What does it matter? They are neither of them made of gold." This from one of the chief's lieutenants. The chief turned to the Doctor as though to give him the opportunity to dispute his man's claim.

"I would dispute that most earnestly," the Doctor said. "The Empress of Huiam herself awaits the arrival of this creature. I am her servant in this task. She would pay an incomparable sum for our release."

"How much?" the leader said.

"You have heard Huiam? You have heard of the Empress and Piufenh and the Eternal Palace? You know of the riches of those places? Well, you could name your price and she would meet it without batting an eye, for it would not be a tenth of her worth, such is her fortune. How much? Enough for each of you to build a palace in this desert, I have no doubt."

The leader considered this for a time, looking hard at the Doctor as though trying to discern what truth there was in his words. He arrived at a decision at last and motioned his men to open the cage where the Minotaur was kept, and then had them lead him by the chains that still bound his wrists. After so long trapped within that prison, the Minotaur was unsteady on his feet, and he fell to his knees with a cry, only to find a sword at his throat, pressed there by the chief, who turned to the Doctor.

"Prove your words," he said. "Make him speak."

The Doctor swallowed and spoke to the Minotaur in the barbarian tongue they shared. "My dear friend, our lives, as you no doubt realize, are in the balance here. You must speak or we shall both perish. Speak to me in this tongue, for they may know some of mine, and we need to take care."

The Minotaur hesitated, thinking for a moment and enjoying the increasing tension he could feel from his former captor. Did he care whether he lived or died, he asked himself, for only a few months ago he had wanted nothing else but to escape this sorrowful realm? It seemed he did after all, for he trembled at the idea of death. But he also knew he wanted to be free of the chains the Doctor had put him in and that now was the chance to see that guaranteed.

"When we escape these bonds, you shall never put them upon me again," he said, and could hear the Doctor sigh in ecstatic relief.

"My word," the Doctor breathed to him, and turned to the bandits, who had muttered at each other in awe at the deep and powerful voice of the beast. "My friend wishes to thank you for your mercy. You see, my good friends. He is the true article and I am as good as my word."

•••

The Minotaur and Doctor Eid were chained together, arm to arm and neck to neck, and led by the bandits deeper and deeper into the wild and rocky hills from whence they had emerged. They walked throughout the day, the Minotaur marking the time by the way the sun shone upon him, the bandits setting a hard pace and rarely stopping. Once they had left the road and disappeared into the hills, the bandits relaxed and became jovial, shouting and teasing each other, celebrating the good fortune of their raid. Beside him, the Doctor muttered a series of repeated phrases under his breath. The Minotaur could not make out what he was saying, whether he was offering prayers or curses to his gods.

By day's end both captives were parched and exhausted, barely able to keep on their feet. When the bandit chieftain called a halt for the day, Doctor Eid fell to his knees, gasping so desperately the Minotaur thought he was weeping.

"You had better have more strength than that, or I have placed my fate in the hands of the wrong man."

When the Doctor had recovered himself he laughed bitterly. "My friend, my strength lies in more ethereal matters. The corporeal defy me often. This shall be a trial as I have never suffered, but fear not – I shall talk us free of it before long."

"We shall see," the Minotaur said.

The chieftain, hearing the two of them conversing, came over and leveled his sword at the Doctor. "What is the beast saying? There shall be no secrets among us now that we are friends."

"Ah, well," the Doctor said, "Naturally. As to that, he was merely chiding me for my weakness after one day's hard work."

"He is a fearsome creature," the chieftain said.

"You need have no fear. He responds to my command, so long as we are both well kept he will not turn against you."

"It is a wonder that anyone was able to blind him."

"He invited the wrath of a god."

The chieftain raised an eye at this. "Is that so? What god is this?"

The Doctor shrugged and then raised himself to his feet so that he might look the bandit in the eye. "I am not familiar with it. A barbarian god, you understand."

The chieftain spat on the ground in response.

"How do you think some a creature as this came to be? The gods had a hand in it, surely."

"Not my gods."

"No, nor mine. We have gods worthy of the name, you and I. This beast, though, comes from a land of fallen gods. They have so fallen that the result is this, congress between a god and a beast."

The chieftain spat again and uttered a curse in the direction of the Minotaur. "He should be put to death. He is an abomination before nature."

"He is an abomination surely, but I would hesitate to put him to death. A fallen god is a god nonetheless, and he has some of their powers, to be sure."

The chieftain considered this a moment. "So long as the Empress pays us the coin promised, the creature lives."

The Doctor nodded and smiled grimly, falling back to ground as soon as the chieftain had walked away. "We are in good hands," he said to the Minotaur. "We are in good hands."

The Minotaur considered this in silence. The Doctor seemed to lose his conviction after that, falling into a miserable contemplation, muttering to himself again. His foul mood was only relieved when the one of bandits brought them both a bit of boiled grain to eat. When they had each scraped their bowls clean, the bandit passed them a skin filled with water, which they emptied between them. That bandit sat down to keep watch on them, another man leaving the comfort of the fire to act as a sentinel somewhere in the darkness.

They passed a frigid night on the ground, the air so cold they could see their breath, and as a result their sleep was fitful. Each time he started awake from his temporary slumber, the Doctor would cast a wary glance around at his captors. Every time the man on watch was alert and vigilant, his fellows all asleep around the dimming fire. He got up to urinate once, moving as far away from the Minotaur and the bandit as his chains would allow him, and when he glanced back toward the fire he saw that his guard had risen to his feet and had his sword in his hands.

The next day was agony for both the Doctor and the Minotaur, stiff from the previous day's exertion and a night spent upon that rocky ground. The bandits fed them again and it was during this meal that a cry went up from the sentinel, and soon they were joined by three other men. The Doctor immediately recognized one of them as one of the merchants who had been part of the caravan. He cried out in disgust and hatred, drawing a thin smile and a nod from his former compatriot. The other two men were unfamiliar to him – no doubt they had acted as intermediaries between the bandits and merchant, letting them know where the caravan was and when the time to strike would be ripe.

The chieftain and the merchant embraced and the merchant said, "Quite the feast, was it not?"

"It was as you promised."

"Good. You have everything ready? My men have the gold."

"All is good, except for these two."

The merchant frowned. "What is the problem? And why did you keep this one alive?"

"That one speaks for the beast," the chieftain said. "Our agreement there does not stand."

"What do you mean? What has this fool told you?" the merchant said, striding over to the Doctor, his hand grasping the pommel of the dagger at his belt.

The bandit standing watch over the Doctor and the Minotaur intercepted him with a shake of his head and a cold stare.

"The creature can speak," the chieftain said, not having stirred from where he stood. "And he translates for him. He is a servant of the Empress herself and she will pay far more than you for the return of these two."

The merchant laughed. "Is that what he told you? Fools. If he is a servant of the empress then I am the Sultan of Teherul."

"I considered that he might be lying. He had great reason, his life was forfeit otherwise. But it is no matter. The creature can speak, I have heard him. He is worth far more than we agreed and I will not give him up for that pittance."

The merchant threw his hands in air and sighed loudly. "Let me guess, you cannot understand what the creature says. It is probably some gibberish that this man has taught him. A simulacrum of a man is all."

The Doctor struggled to his feet, wincing as he did so at the aches and pains that plagued him. "My good friends," he said, "I hesitate to interject myself into your discussion—"

"Then leave off, fool," the merchant said.

"Let him speak," the chieftain said, not taking his eyes from the merchant's.

"Many thanks," the Doctor said, offering a small bow. "As I say, I hesitate to interject, but this is a discussion that I have a certain investment in, so to speak. You both claim that I had every reason to lie about the beast, and that is true. But is it not also the case that I have the most to lose from falsehood? What does lying gain me? A moment's respite from your blade, for inevitably you must discover my deception. If the beast is a fraud and the Empress does not ransom us, you can still kill me and sell it to the highest bidder. I will have gained nothing but a few miserable days as your prisoner."

"There is reason there." The chieftain nodded.

"Don't listen to this nonsense," the merchant said. "A few miserable days is more than he would have had otherwise. Besides, we have an agreement."

"Our agreement does not include this creature."

The merchant spat with rage. "How can it not? Have I not always treated you with honor?"

At a glance from the chieftain, the bandits seized the merchant's men, disarming them and forcing them to their knees while keeping blades poised at their throats. Seeing this, the merchant snarled and drew his own sword, burying it deep in the gut of the bandit who had been standing watch on the Doctor and the Minotaur. Before the other bandits had a chance to react, the merchant stepped toward the Minotaur and leveled a sword at his throat.

"Release my men, or this creature dies and no one shall enjoy the riches he will bring."

The chieftain looked from the dying bandit to the merchant without expression and raised his hand to signal his men to release their prisoners. The merchant smiled grimly. "Now we return to the matter of our negotiation for this creature."

He did not have the opportunity to complete his thought, for the Minotaur, moving with a speed that astonished all present, knocked aside the merchant's sword and seized him by throat. The merchant's eyes bulged in astonishment and his lips formed words that his throat gave no sound to. The Minotaur held him for a moment, seeming to stare into the man's eyes with his dead ones, before snapping his neck with a twist of his hands, the terrible sound of the bones breaking causing everyone else to wince. The merchant went limp in his hands, his bladder and intestines emptying, and the Minotaur tossed the body to the ground.

The merchant's two compatriots were beheaded even as they stared at the corpse of their master. The chieftain glanced at their bodies to see that the work was done to his satisfaction and then approached the Minotaur, being sure to stay beyond the reach of his arms.

"We shall have to keep an eye on this one – and at a safe distance," he said, and laughed.

•••

Having dispatched with the rest of the merchant's men and collected not only the spoils of their raid on the caravan but the gold that had been intended to pay for it, the bandits set off toward Huiam to ransom the Doctor and the Minotaur. Rather than travel the roads that the caravan had been on, they stayed in the rocky desert highlands, where they knew the terrain well and could disappear at a moment if need be. As they traveled they encountered other bands of confederates who joined them, for there were plenty of spoils to be shared and neither the beast nor the armies of Huiam were to be trifled with.

The bandits saw that the Doctor and the beast were well cared for, not wanting to risk losing their fortune to the vagaries of travel. They were kept chained together and mealtimes developed into an elaborate ritual where one bandit would bring their food while two others trained arrows upon the beast. Even as they journeyed, the bandits on horseback leading their two prisoners walking and stumbling behind, two men kept arrows notched in their bows, ready to loose at the first sign of trouble from the Minotaur.

"A pity you had to demonstrate your faculties," the Doctor remarked during one of the breaks the chieftain had called. "We might have used that to our advantage if they had remained unsuspecting."

"I thought your tongue was going to loose our bonds," the Minotaur said to him, laughter in his voice. While their forced march had been hard on the Doctor, the Minotaur seemed only to gain in strength as the days went on. His steps grew only more assured the longer he walked, his senses and his intuition now so attuned to his blindness that he felt certain he could identify where all the bandits and their horses were at any given moment.

"My good friend," the Doctor said, "do not let our present bleak circumstances confuse your senses. Here in this desert we are at their mercy, there can be no doubt, for this is their world. But once we reach Huiam, the advantage turns in our favor. Those are my people and I am known there. Now we must be patient and marshal our strength."

They walked for so many days the Minotaur lost count, passing from the desert to a verdant highland, a place of forests and afternoon rains. According to the Doctor they were nearing Huiam, this being one of the kingdoms that paid tribute to the empire. Having left their homeland, the bandits grew ever more wary, forming a sort of phalanx on horseback around their prized possessions as they traveled, and every approaching person was treated with suspicion. They took a circuitous route, staying as far from populated areas as they could, the better to escape notice and avoid having the Minotaur becoming known.

Their caution proved to be for naught, for a local baron caught wind of their passage and knew that such a caravan of well-armed foreigners must be protecting some fabulous treasure, and he sought to take it for himself.

Calling on his retainers, he gathered a force of men and confronted the bandits, demanding that they pay an exorbitant custom for passing through his land. This delighted the Doctor, for he felt certain that they would fall into the hands of the baron, whom he could easily influence. As he told the Minotaur, all inhabitants of these tributary lands were desperate above all to be seen as civilized and cultured as an Huiamite.

Though the tax imposed was costly, the bandits were able to pay it with ease from the gold and the spoils they had taken from the merchant, the chieftain justifying doing so by saying they would more than make their fortune back in the selling of the beast. The baron was so taken aback by the bandits' ability to meet his demands that he assumed they must be representatives of a barbarian kingdom and dared not press them for more, lest he find himself embroiled in a conflict he could not hope to win. And so they passed from the highlands to the mountains that marked the border with Huiam. There they halted, much to the Doctor's frustration, sending two representatives into the empire to find an administrator or lord who would speak for the Empress and meet their demands.

"We must go to Huiam," Doctor Eid said to the chieftain. "No one will pay any mind to some barbarian who comes in speaking of a mystical beast. They will listen to me."

"You say you are known in this land. Will they not come for you if they hear your life is at stake?"

The Doctor tried to convince him otherwise, saying that, no matter if he was the Empress' consort himself, the imperial administrators would ignore any barbarians who came before them. Try as he might, though, the chieftain could not be persuaded and they all settled in to await the return of the two men.

"What word, I wonder, will they bring with them?" the Minotaur said to the Doctor.

"A death sentence," the Doctor said miserably.

"Do not lose hope just yet. What are those flowers I smell?"

"Some manner of athahea. Foul-smelling things."

The Minotaur smiled. "I thought as much. We have the same plant in Rheadd. And there are a great many of them, am I right?"

"The whole valley is covered in them."

"Good. I am certain I heard bees as well, collecting pollen from them, which means there must be honey nearby. You must get the bandits to eat of that honey. We will see if your tongue is as worthy as you believe."

"What will eating honey do?" The Doctor frowned.

"Taste it yourself and you shall find out."

"Very well," the Doctor said, still sounding skeptical. "I shall endeavor to have them taste the fruit."

When the chieftain sent some of his men out into the valley and the surrounding hills to forage for food, the Doctor intercepted him and asked if he could have his men bring back any honey they might find.

"Perhaps enough for all your men," the Doctor said hurriedly when the chieftain looked ready to refuse his request. "My stomach has been ailing me these past days and it is well known that the honey from these flowers has a restorative effect. It brings vitality to any man who tastes of it."

"Is that so?"

"Quite, quite, my good friend," the Doctor said. "If it is not too much to trouble you and your men, I would be in your debt, more so than now, if that is possible."

"I hardly think so," the chieftain said, but he told his men to bring honey if they could find it, and when they returned that evening from their foraging mission they had some that they had collected and put into a ceramic jug. The Doctor thanked the men and the chieftain profusely for what they had done and urged them all to eat it, saying that he would take the smallest morsel for himself.

"You will take whatever we give you," one of the bandits said to him.

"Of course. Of course, as you say, my good friend," the Doctor said, bowing his head.

The honey was added to the boiled grain that each man received a ration of and served to everyone, including the two prisoners. The Doctor thanked the bandits profusely for their kindness. He set his bowl aside and watched as the bandits ate their portion. The Minotaur ate his without hesitation.

"What manner of poison is this if you feel free to taste of it?" the Doctor said to the beast, gesturing at his bowl.

"The effect is cumulative," the Minotaur said. "I would need to eat much more than you or any of these others to feel it. But all these men will be suffering before the night is out."

"I will not partake, then," the Doctor said.

"Good, we shall need to be ready to act once their suffering begins."

The chieftain, however, noticed the Doctor had not eaten his portion, and approached him. "You demand this favor and now that it has been granted you do not even deign to offer a taste. I would ask you why?"

"My friend, my stomach, I fear, is too weak. I will not keep the restorative down enough for it to do me any good."

"How do you know, unless you try?"

"It is not the first time I have suffered from such a malady," the Doctor said, offering a commiserating grin. "It has troubled me throughout the years, I am afraid. An affliction of the nerves."

"So you say," the chieftain said. "Each of us has eaten of it, including your beast, and the man who requested it has tasted not a drop. One wonders. This troublesome malady appears to be invisible as well. I have no evidence of any suffering on your part."

"I assure you—" the Doctor began to say.

"All the same, I would feel better at ease if you were to taste of it," the chieftain said, picking up the full bowl and handing it to the Doctor.

He swallowed and nodded, taking the bowl from the chieftain's hand and eating the now cold gruel. The sweetness of the honey came through strongly and he nearly wretched at its taste. The chieftain waited until he had scraped the bowl clean and managed a smile before returning to where his men were gathered about the fire.

"In the next few days, I expect the return of our brothers and we shall see to the truth of your other claims," he called as he went.

The Doctor attempted a jaunty reply but the words fell dead on his lips, such was his worry about what was soon to befall him now that he had ingested the poisoned honey. He could feel his hands beginning to tremble, and he had to hide them in his robes so they did not attract the attention of the bandit who kept watch upon he and Minotaur. His eyes stayed on the valley's horizon, where the last rays of the day's sun burnt across the sky, watching until they had disappeared and the darkness seized the heavens.

"What shall happen to me?" he asked the Minotaur as he lay down to sleep on the unforgiving ground.

The voice that replied was vast and deep and, the Doctor thought, portending doom. "You will know when it comes."

•••

The Doctor was in fact the first to suffer the delirium brought on by the poisoned honey. His dreams were filled with fantastic and tormented images that he could scarcely make sense of, nightmares where he died a thousand deaths. The terror of these dreams became so great that at last he was started awake. The night was cool and silent, the fire nearly down to coals. His stomach lashed about violently, a ship tossed about in a storm. Worried that he was about to vomit, he raised himself up to a sitting position, only to find the world spinning in a gyre round his head.

When he had managed to steady himself, he looked around. The bandits slept untroubled by the dimming fire; he could hear their breathing over the dying crackle of the flames. But the man who had been tasked with keeping watch on the two prisoners was gone, he realized, which meant this was the moment the Minotaur had spoken of earlier. The Doctor struggled to his feet and turned to the beast to let him know that the time to flee was now, only to find that the Minotaur had disappeared. As he struggled to comprehend how this could have happened, he saw the chains that had bound both of them together lying on the ground at his feet.

Cursing the beast for abandoning him, he lurched forward, trying to flee, his legs seemingly unable to respond to his commands. The darkness seemed to swim with color, shadows and ghosts he assumed, some of them threatening, and he fought to avoid them as he went. He was so focused on avoiding these pitfalls, while trying to move as quietly as possible, his every step sounding like thunderclap to his ears, that he did not notice that he had turned himself around and was now moving directly toward the fire and the sleeping bandits. It was only when he stepped on one of their prone forms, eliciting a shout and a curse from the sleeping man, that he realized his mistake. Compounding his error, he tried to run away, but instead came crashing through the fire and the rest of the slumbering bandits, stumbling and tripping and sending half a dozen men awake.

The Doctor ended up flat on the ground, his face pressed into one of the athahea shrubs. Behind him he could hear shouts as the bandits roused themselves and realized that their prisoners had escaped. He forced himself to turn over and sit up and was in time to see one of the men, lurching about just as he had, fall into the fire, his clothes catching alight. The bandit screamed terribly and the smell of burnt flesh filled the air as the man thrashed about on the ground trying to douse the flames, succeeding only in keeping them alight as he rolled back into the fire again and again.

None of the other bandits came to their fellow's aid; instead his screams and the flames seemed to send them into a state of uncontrolled panic. They ran with the same contorted gait as he, stumbling and falling as they went, off into the darkness. Two of them came near where the Doctor lay and he shouted in surprise, for they had been utterly transformed. They were horned beasts, just like the Minotaur, except their eyes shone like fire in the darkness and their breath smelled of smoke. He scurried away from them, weeping as he went, begging the creatures to grant him mercy for ever imprisoning their brother.

After crawling for what seemed like hours, he collapsed in exhaustion and fell asleep, the night quiet around him. When he awoke the darkness still held sway, and he rolled onto his back and saw the stars and moon still bright above. Looking about him, he realized he could see no sign of the bandits' fire, nor could he hear any of them. No doubt they felt as he did, exhausted and racked by agonizing pain in their stomachs. Every moment brought a fresh assault, like a tremor rippling across his body, that would subside and offer some scant relief, only to be replaced by the next a second later.

Was he fated to die in this place, he wondered, so near to his home and his people? It seemed a fitting end, he thought miserably, for one who had driven himself into exile in a mad search for glory, only to be thwarted in that desire just as it seemed within his grasp. A fitting end for a fool, which he undoubtedly was – no better than the barbarians he had lived with all these long years.

Around him the forest stirred and he had visions of panthers and bears stalking him through the forest. A creature emerged from the brush and loomed above him, its form blotting out the sky above. The Doctor held his breath and closed his eyes, bracing himself for the death blow that he felt certain was moments away from arriving.

"Come," the Minotaur whispered, kneeling beside him, his head so near that the Doctor could feel his warm breath. "We must be far from here if we are to assure ourselves of escape."

"Do with me as you wish," the Doctor said. "I am deserving."

"I have need of you," the Minotaur said, picking him up. "If I am to go to Huiam I shall need someone to be my voice, for you never did finish your lessons."

The Doctor smiled, unable to stop himself from weeping. "Thank you, my good friend," he said. The beast offered no reply. Already he had begun to make his way out of the valley.

•••

The Minotaur could not say exactly why he had returned for Doctor Eid. It was not that he felt any great compulsion to go to Huiam. He was certain he could craft an existence for himself in whatever kingdom he now found himself in, all his journeys had proven that much at least, and while he had been intrigued by all that the good Doctor had told him of his home, he suspected that, as with the many other subjects on which the Doctor found himself speaking, he should not be taken at face value. The man had imprisoned him, after all – a forgivable offense given the assumptions he had made about his innate nature, but declining to release him once he had shown himself to be a man of reason was something not easily forgotten.

Yet their shared captivity had drawn him closer to the rogue, and the days of whispered plotting and worry had succeeded in creating a sense of camaraderie, which he had been unable to shake free of after he had struck down the guard and extracted himself from his chains. He had thought he had done right by the Doctor in setting him free as well, but the farther he had slipped away in the darkness the more his conscience had worn at him. The Minotaur knew the state the Doctor would be in once the honey had begun to affect him and he knew that no escape would be possible. And there he would remain to fall prey to the bandits as they recovered and realized that their prized possession had been taken from them. It did not take much imagination to understand what they would do to the Doctor in that situation.

So he had returned and collected Doctor Eid and started for Huiam, reasoning that it was as good a place as any to go, and even better to be traveling with a native who was in his debt. The Doctor had more or less recovered from his symptoms the following day, and they made good time, leaving the highlands behind for the mountains. They stayed to the main roads, thinking that the bandits would not expect them to and would, by their nature, avoid them regardless. The going was easier for the Minotaur as well, for though he had developed a preternatural ability to move about sightless on almost any terrain, it was still much easier for him on a regular path.

Naturally, they attracted attention wherever they went, the more so because after so many days spent under the sword of the bandits, sleeping on the cold ground and subsisting on gruel, the Doctor appeared to be a man come from great poverty, not the finely cultured and educated man he had looked before. Next to the awe inspired by the sight of such a magnificent creature as the Minotaur, the Doctor seemed a miserable human being, hardly worthy of being in such company. When people approached the two of them to inquire as to who they were, it was to the Minotaur they spoke to, and they laughed at the Doctor when he tried to spin some grand tale of the hardship, triumph and friendship that lay between them.

They were not molested as they went, unlike in so

many of the other places the Minotaur had passed through, and they quickly made their way through the various villages that were scattered along the pass through the mountains. "Leaf-chewers," the Doctor referred to the locals derisively, after their habit of chewing a local herb at all times. But it was a peaceable land, filled with generous souls, and they journeyed without incident and with full bellies, until they descended out of the mountains and into Huiam proper.

The Doctor spoke unceasingly as soon as they entered his ancestral land, excitedly telling the Minotaur of all there was to see, describing a place of endless marvels. A feast for all the senses. The Minotaur could not help but smile at his friend's enthusiasm now that they were well and truly free of the bandits and he was returned home. The Doctor led them to the nearest city, a place called Idyhin, where he said there was an academy, some of whose members he was acquainted with. They could provide them aid and help him spread the word of his great scientific discovery.

"We will be on the road to Piufenh before the week is out," he said to the beast.

The Minotaur cared little where they journeyed. He was curious to see if the good Doctor had friends of influence or if that too had been mere bluster. Regardless, so long as the tongue of these people was foreign to him, he had decided to follow the Doctor wherever he led. After that he would see. If these were a people of science and philosophy as the Doctor kept telling him, then he had no doubt opportunities would present themselves, for there would no shortage of people who would be interested in meeting him and hearing his tales.

It was while they were on the way through Idyhin's winding streets, which felt to the Minotaur as though they were turning about in endless circles, that they encountered the two bandits who the chieftain had sent to find someone willing to pay the Doctor's promised ransom. With them was an Administrator and his small guard. When the bandits spotted the beast wandering free down the road, they shouted and had the soldiers draw their blades and surround both the Minotaur and the Doctor.

"My good friend," the Doctor said, speaking directly to the Administrator, "this is all a terrible misunderstanding."

"Is that so?" the Administrator said. "These men claim that you have promised them some coin and that they had seized you and this creature until someone was able to pay your debt."

"Utter nonsense, I assure you. These men are brigands of the worst sort. I was part of a caravan of half a dozen of Huiam's finest merchants and we were attacked by these bandits. Everyone was killed but me, and I was taken prisoner."

One of the bandits began to protest what the Doctor had said, but the Administrator silenced him with a raised hand. "Subject," he said to the Doctor, "why were you spared by these men when all the others were killed?"

"Mere serendipity. They sought this creature." He gestured at the Minotaur, who stood uneasily listening to what was being said, understanding only the odd phrase. "And I managed to convince them that he was valueless to them without me."

"What value does the creature have?"

"Is it not obvious? He is a stupendous creation, a marvel of the age. I was returning with him to Huiam – I had plans to display him at the Academy, for there is much of the world that can be learned from him – when we were assailed by these fiends. The creature can speak, I can demonstrate. Sadly, he only knows a barbarian tongue of which I have become conversant in."

"I see," the Administrator said, eyeing the creature. "Is it not dangerous?"

The Doctor shook his head. "How do you think we escaped from these bandit fellows? They let down their guard for a moment and he killed them all. Tore them limb from limb. A terrifying sight, as you can imagine. Fortunately, I can command the creature, to a degree, but I had actually planned on seeking you out to see if you might aid me in caging him. He should not be loose upon the streets."

The Administrator considered this, looking from the Minotaur to the Doctor to the bandits. At last, his decision made, he turned to the bandits. "This man is a subject of Huiam. You have no claim to him. This beast you may have a claim to, but you have provided no proof beyond your word."

"Neither has he," one of the bandits said.

"He is a subject of Huiam," the Administrator continued. "You are a barbarian. His word counts for more in the eyes of the law. If you have more proof to offer you may pursue your claims in the Court of Huiam, provided you can find a subject of Empress to represent you. I bid you good day, gentleman."

The Administrator turned from the flabbergasted bandits and motioned to the Doctor to follow him. He did, calling for the Minotaur to come. As they went, the Administrator's guard discreetly formed a phalanx around the Doctor and the Minotaur, their hands on their swords, ready to respond at a word from the Administrator. He sent a boy ahead of them with a message so that when they arrived at the imperial offices of Idyhin a cage had been set atop a caravan, not unlike the one the Doctor had imprisoned the Minotaur in previously, and a large number of soldiers stood ready to assist.

The Minotaur had noticed the guard surrounding them as they walked down the street, but it had not aroused his suspicions. The Doctor had offered no comment on the matter, and so he had simply assumed it was standard practice, or that the Administrator was ensuring that they were protected from the bandits. It was only when they came to the Imperial Offices that he realized something was wrong. The Doctor disappeared from his side and he could hear the phalanx of guards drawing their swords and leveling them at him. They were joined by the waiting soldiers, so that he found himself surrounded by an untold number of men.

He snarled in disbelief and rage and could hear the men closest to him step back in fear.

"Come, my good friend," the Doctor said to him. "You always knew how this was to end. I seized you and you are mine."

"I am a man of reason, just as you are. You know that."

"You are a barbarian and a beast. Under Huiam law I have the right to claim you. If you wish to dispute it you may do so in Court. But you must find someone to represent you, and my word weighs more heavily than yours here."

"To think that I spared your life."

"I am eternally grateful. Forever in your debt, really," the Doctor said. "I shall see you well treated. Now, please, do not make this difficult. These men will not hesitate to kill you."

The Minotaur was silent, clenching and unclenching his hands and grinding his teeth in fury. He tried to determine whether or not he could get through the phalanx of soldiers to where the Doctor stood, thinking that he would not mind dying so long as the other man suffered the same fate. It would be a futile attempt, he realized; there were simply too many men arrayed against him and he could not be absolutely certain where the Doctor was now or where he would flee to once he launched his attack. His shoulders sagged and his breath left his chest in a mournful sigh.

"That is good, my friend," the Doctor said. "You have made the wise choice. You shall not regret it."

The Minotaur climbed into the cage, refusing to speak, thinking only that he would see that the Doctor rued his betrayal.

•••

The Minotaur refused to speak another word in the presence of the Doctor, even as he arranged engagements at the Academies of Idyhin and some other nearby cities. If he was to be treated as no more than a beast then he would act as one, he decided, and let the Doctor's claims that he was a wondrous creature be proven false. He sat in his cage in glowering silence, his anger palpable and vibrating to the audiences of the lecture hall or salon as Doctor Eid spoke of his amazing discovery and the strange, barbaric land he had come from. The Minotaur tried not to listen to these speeches, tried to will himself into oblivion in those moments, but he failed, especially when the questions from the audience began, and gradually he started to understand something of what was being said, making his slavery all the worse.

His plan to deny the Doctor the value of his speech, the wonder that it would no doubt inspire, failed utterly. The Doctor's lectures were a huge success, he was praised and feted everywhere they went, and soon he had received an invite from the Academy in Piufenh to display the creature there and lecture on all his travels. It was almost not to be believed, so rapid was the Doctor's ascension among the respectable and learned men of Huiam. How long the Doctor had imagined such moments of triumph as he was experiencing?

"It is as though my whole life has been in preparation for this time," he told the Minotaur on more than one occasion. He could not resist speaking to the creature, especially as they spent all their days together, his success inextricably bound to the sullen and mute beast. To return from his long self-imposed exile and to be feted as one of the great explorers of the age was beyond belief, especially after the hard months of imprisonment he had endured at the hands of the bandits. This too became part of his tale, along with the discovery of the beast, though that part was transformed, along with his years spent selling vials of colored water to unsuspecting barbarians, to something more befitting the man of learning and culture he aspired to be.

The Doctor's joy at these developments was tempered by his need to keep the beast within his sight at all times. All depended on the creature, he knew, and he trusted no one, not the philosophers and nobles who came to his talks, and certainly not the Minotaur himself. It became an obsession that he could not relieve himself of, even for a moment. He slept beside the cage, even when the Academies forced him to use their stables to store the creature, took all his meals in sight of it, and he insisted that every soiree and function that followed his lectures be held in the same hall where the Minotaur was displayed. He would rarely stray from beside the cage even during these celebrations, nor would he allow even the most esteemed and honored members of the Academies to get too close, claiming that the beast was unpredictable and not to be trusted. For all the praise he received, and as much as he believed he was deserving of it and more, he knew that without the Minotaur he would be but another rogue adventurer returned home with a half-believed tale to tell.

As soon as he received word of the Piufenh Academy's invitation, the Doctor set to making the arrangements for their journey, spending coin he did not have. He hired a substantial guard to ensure that the Minotaur could neither escape nor be taken from him, as well as buying himself the finest of clothes so that his reappearance in the imperial capital would be as splendorous as he had always imagined. To allay these expenses he stopped in every town and city along the way, delivering his lecture and displaying the creature to great excitement, perfecting the story he would tell once he reached the imperial capital.

It took them two weeks to reach the capital, and by then word of the good Doctor and his wondrous beast had spread even among the commoners of the city. A great crowd met him at the gates of Piufenh upon his arrival. He passed within, surrounded by this swelling retinue that conducted him to the Academy, where he stood atop the balcony where public lectures were given and promised that there would be public showings of the beast so that all might see it. That night, having had no time to rest and recover from his journey, the Doctor spoke before the learned men of the Academy, many of them the same honored thinkers he had idolized in his childhood, and was received with rapturous praise.

After his talk, and the soiree that followed, the Doctor, still electric from the excitement of all the commendations he had been given by the gathered luminaries, was unable to sleep. He paced about the Cabinet of Wonder, where the Academy had placed the Minotaur's cage, giving it a position of honor amongst its many awe-inspiring exhibits. There was a tentacled sea monster here, carefully preserved in a brine, the skeleton of two-headed man there and many other strange and malformed creatures. The Minotaur was at one with them, an oddity of nature, singular and amazing. He was oblivious to his surroundings, though, lying on the floor of his hated prison, listening to the footsteps of the man who had betrayed him.

At last the Doctor could contain his excitement no longer and he approached the cage. "One of the Empress' philosophers was in attendance this evening," he said, speaking in the barbarian tongue they shared.

The Minotaur did not stir from where he lay.

"My good friend, I am certain we will be asked before her. After that there will be public audiences. We shall be the talk of all the empire."

The Doctor was overcome by the energy that was coursing through him, all his thoughts colliding at once in his mind, and he could not stop himself from moving. He left the Minotaur to go inspect a fossil of an unfathomably massive and elongated lizard, the Dragon of Bui, named so for the man who had discovered its remains. The beast, Doctor Eid knew, would be named after him in all the books that were sure to be written on the subject. He would need to think of a proper name for it, something more descriptive than "beast" or "creature." The thought of such a task delighted him as well. There would be volumes to be written, and perhaps a Society of Discovery to found.

He returned to the cage, where the creature's breathing had subsided into a steady rhythm. He wondered if the beast was asleep. The Doctor smiled, thinking now of the days to come, the triumphs that would fill the hours, and he whispered, so as not to wake his captive, "My good friend, when this is done, when I have been justly rewarded and given a post here at the Academy, I shall free you. You can go where you please."

The Minotaur was not asleep, and he heard the good Doctor's words. They left him cold with rage, only deepening the hatred he felt for this man. He would accept nothing from the Doctor, not even freedom. He would find a means to push aside this proffered hand and spit upon his face.

•••

After a fortnight in which the Doctor gave lectures to all the learned academicians of Piufenh, as well as many of the noble and merchant classes, the wealthiest and most influential people of the Empire, an Imperial Messenger arrived at the Cabinet of Wonder requesting his presence, and that of beast, at the Eternal Palace. The Doctor could not contain his excitement, for the rest of the day he talked endlessly to the unresponsive Minotaur, even as he prepared for his talk that evening. When the appointed hour arrived the Imperial Messenger returned, along with a dozen men from the Imperial Guard dressed in their azure robes, to escort them to the Palace.

Once they had passed through the four walls that

guarded the Palace, they were led through an endless labyrinth of gardens to a broad hall somewhere within the complex where the court had been gathered, at the head of which, atop a broad and high dais, sat the Empress herself. She was dressed ornately in a many-layered scarlet robe, her face painted a chalky white except for her eyes, which were circled black. Her hair was tied into ringlets set in a fantastical arrangement that seemed as though it would topple her head if she but moved. She did not, though, holding herself harshly upright in her chair, staring out at those assembled with a stern look upon her face, ignoring the ministrations of the eunuch attendants at her feet. The Doctor trembled as he approached her, yet when he came near he saw that she was startlingly young, no more than a girl.

That reassured him momentarily, but her eyes cut through him, dismissing him in an instant, and when she commanded him to begin his speech he had not yet regained his equilibrium.

"My good friends, your high and graceful one," he began, the words sounding ridiculous in his mouth. He cleared his throat and began again. "Most exalted one and honored luminaries. Good friends. I bring before you one of the wonders of the age. A wondrous beast, part bull and part man, born in the barbarian empire of Rheadd – the result, many there say, of illicit congress between a god and a woman of high birth."

Having found the rhythm of his tale, the Doctor proceeded in earnest, elaborating on the Minotaur's life and adding such flourishes as he felt were necessary. He had begun to tell his own story of the lands he had been to, the other wonders he had seen, the trials he had endured and the knowledge that he had returned with, when the Empress interrupted him with a raised hand.

"Yes, most exalted and graceful?" he said, his mouth dry.

"Release the beast from it's cage, good Doctor. I wish

to inspect it more closely."

The Doctor was taken aback by the request. "Most exalted, ah," he said, "I would recommend against such a course. That is, it would be unwise to release the beast. He is not to be trusted free."

"And why not, good Doctor?"

"Well, most exalted, I cannot guarantee to you that he will behave according to proper courtly manners as would befit a man. He is both violent and dangerous."

"Are you saying my Guard cannot handle it?" the Empress said, arching one eyebrow. "I find that hard to believe. Besides, is it not half a beast and half a man? If it is a bull then it can be tamed, and it is a man then it can be reasoned with. In either case it can be freed, at least for the moment."

The Doctor did not dare argue further with the Empress – not with twenty of her elite Guard standing armed and at the ready. They moved in to surround the cage as the Empress stepped down from the dais, providing a shield in case the Doctor's concerns proved real. With trembling hands he unlocked the cage's door, unable to look at the guard or the Empress.

"Do not forget my promise," the Doctor whispered to the beast, who gave no indication that he heard. He swung the door open and stepped back, keeping himself well clear of the space the guard had left in front of the cage.

At first it seemed the Minotaur would not leave his prison, though the Doctor had clearly seen him cock his head at the sound of the door swinging wide. He had spent the entirety of the Doctor's talk sprawled upon the floor of the cage, not bothering to raise his head even at their entrance, which had been accompanied by a fanfare of trumpets. A hush settled over everyone gathered – the guards, the courtiers and servants and assembled dignitaries and nobles, all seemed to be holding their breath collectively as they awaited the beast's first movement. Only the Empress seemed imperturbable, her face betraying no emotion as she awaited the creature.

Like an actor who could sense the emotions of his audience, the Minotaur waited until the tension was almost unbearable before rising to his feet in a languorous motion, taking a step toward the door of the cage and then pausing as though tasting the air. As he watched this calculated display, the Doctor felt his stomach fall away and blood rush from his face. The beast was plotting something, he could tell. But without him to translate his barbarian utterings, the Doctor tried to reassure himself, what voice could the Minotaur give to his plight? The Guard would stop him from doing anything foolish as well, he told himself, though none of his reasoning seemed to do anything to ease his worry.

The Minotaur stepped out and away from the cage, approaching the men arrayed against him, all of whom cringed and grasped the hilts of their swords. His size, the odor that clung to him, even the sound of his breathing – all of it overwhelmed those near him, except the Empress, who pushed her way through her Guard so that she stood near enough the beast to touch him. The Minotaur stood as she inspected him, going around him twice, the fascination and excitement she felt written plain on her face.

"I had not thought such a wonder could exist," she said to herself, the commanding tone she habitually used absent.

"Nor I, most exalted," the Minotaur said to her in her own tongue. "It is an honor to meet one of whom I have heard such extraordinary things."

The room became, if such a thing were possible, even more silent and still following the beast's words. The Empress took a step back from the Minotaur, the better to look into his dead eyes. "It speaks. Truly a wonder. Why did you not speak before? Why did you say nothing?"

The last remark she directed at the Doctor, who found himself unable to respond, so flabbergasted was he by the

Minotaur's apparent ability to speak in a civilized tongue.

"I swore a vow, most exalted, that I would not speak until I was released from my prison," the Minotaur said. "That man calls me a beast, but I am no such thing. I am a man of reason and learning. I was taught by the greatest philosophers of Rheadd and was a contestant in their greatest tournaments. I was forced into this cage against my will, after having saved this man's life from bandits who had captured us."

"Is what he says true?" The Empress turned to the Doctor, her eyes cold.

"Absolutely not, most exalted – these are the most exorbitant lies I have ever heard. This beast is violent and unpredictable, as I said. He is not to be trusted."

"He does not appear violent to me, good Doctor."

The Doctor, flustered by the Empress' questioning, stepped toward her, his hands out, pleading, and was seized by two of the Guards nearest him, their grips tight on his arms.

"Not only does he not appear violent, good Doctor," the Empress continued, "he speaks. A fact you neglected to mention. To anyone, in any of your talks at our fine Academies. And he is learned, clearly, experienced in the ways of court. Hardly a barbarian, I would say."

"Oh, but he is," the Doctor said. "He is, most exalted. You must not trust him."

"I am beginning to wonder if I should trust you, good Doctor. You have withheld so much that would have been fruitful for discussion."

"He has withheld more than that, most exalted," the Minotaur said. "He was no explorer and adventurer, leading a life of knowledge and exploration, when I met him. He was a scoundrel and rogue, telling tales and stealing the coins of honest people, preying on their ignorance of the ways of the world. He saw fit to take advantage of me, and though I did much to help him and even considered him a friend, at the first moment opportunity offered it, he betrayed me."

"Lies, most exalted, fiendish lies," the Doctor said. "He would say anything to set himself free."

"I have no doubt of that," the Empress said. "It does not alter the fact that you have most certainly uttered falsehoods in my presence."

The Doctor's entire frame slumped in defeat at the Empress' words, the force of being that had driven him evaporating. All that he had fought for was slipping from his grasp. The blood left his face and he feared he would go faint. He looked, wild-eyed, about the room, feeling as though he could not breathe, ending up staring into the Minotaur's dead eyes, for the beast had glanced unerringly in his direction. The Doctor was certain, though he knew it was impossible, that the beast was staring at him. A small grin seemed to touch the Minotaur's lips and disappear as quickly as it came into existence. The Doctor clenched his fists in rage.

"Tell me," the Empress said to the Minotaur, paying no mind to the Doctor, "why I should trust you. Now that you are free, can you be expected to live a gainful life in our fine Empire? Or will you act as the Doctor expects?"

The Minotaur kneeled before the Empress, lowering his head so that his horns were extended near her hands. "I ask nothing of you, most exalted, or this great Empire, expect to be granted the honor to serve you in whatever way you require. I humbly submit myself to your judgment."

"I am glad to hear you say it," the Empress said with a grave smile. "I shall consider your request."

She was about to say something further but was interrupted by a cry from the Doctor. His fury at the beast, especially after he had supplicated himself before the Empress, offering service that the Doctor had, only moments before, been certain was his to claim, had unhinged him. He was blind to all in the room but the Minotaur – it was as though the Empress, her Guard and all the courtiers had vanished and only he and his nemesis remained in the great hall. He shouted a challenge to the beast, his rage transforming it into an incoherent scream as he charged.

Though there were at least a dozen men near the Doctor who might have been able to intercept him, none of them moved as he started towards the Minotaur. It was as though they could not believe what they were witnessing. No man would attempt such a thing surrounded by the Imperial Guard, not when it assuredly meant his death. The rest of those gathered were unable to react as well, but for a few gasps that seemed to echo across the silent hall. The Empress stepped back, throwing her hands up before her, as though she expected the Doctor to attack her, for what else could the man be about?

Because of the silence and the stillness of everyone else in the room, the Minotaur had no difficulty hearing the Doctor's cry or his sudden approach, and he had no doubt what the man was about. He did not rise to his feet, nor did he make any movement to betray his awareness until the Doctor was upon him. At the last moment he turned his lowered head, so suddenly that the Doctor had no time to alter his course, leveling his horns directly in the man's path. The Doctor impaled himself on them, letting out a mournful cry. This, at last, stirred the Guard to action, and two of the men approached the pair, joined together in their bloody clasp, and executed the Doctor.

There was a long silence as the two guards dragged the Doctor's body free from the Minotaur's horns until the Empress regained her composure and spoke.

"You have proven your worth already," she said, with a significant glance at the assembled Guard. "Do you have a name that I might call you?"

"Among my people I was called Minotaur," he said.

The Empress nodded. "So it shall be, Minotaur. Rise and join the Eternal Court."

•••

In the years that followed the Minotaur became the Empress' constant companion; rarely a day passed at court when the two of them were not seen together. The Minotaur had arrived in the early days of the Empress' rule in Huiam. She had only recently thrown off the shackles of a regency led by several princes, and her control of the realm was still tenuous. Every advisor and every courtier in the palace was allied with one prince or another, all of them plotting to ensnare her in a favorable alliance, through marriage or otherwise, or indebt her to them in some way. The Minotaur had no such ties, except to her, and she had given him his life and freedom, so she felt she could trust him as she could no other. He was an intimidating presence, looming over everyone in court, and the Empress used that to her advantage, always having him at her side when she held audiences. Because of the trust he engendered, he became her messenger to the princes and other nobles, and since they had all witnessed his slaying of the Doctor, none dared trifle with him.

The great matter of the day in the empire was the marriage of the Empress, for the regent princes and other nobles all insisted that she had to marry for the good of the realm – naturally, into one of their families or those of their allies. In the first days of her rule the Empress had declined to consider suitors, claiming that she was too young, both in age and in her rule, to consider such things, but, after the Minotaur was ensconced at court, she agreed to see any suitor sent before her. Many came bearing an endless assortment of gifts and with honeyed words of praise on their lips. They abased themselves at her feet, asking for her hand, and she refused them, as the Minotaur glowered at her side, saying that she was betrothed only to the Empire.

Inevitably, rumors began that she had taken the Minotaur as her lover. Those at court began to refer to him derisively as her pet or worse, though none dared say anything to either of them directly, fearing what the Empress might have the Minotaur do. There was no truth to such talk, but it suited the Empress well enough to have it said, for the whiff of scandal that it created, in addition to her defiance of the princes who sought to control her, endeared her to the populace. It did not hurt that the Imperial Guard, which was composed largely of men of no account and whose support was imperative to her continued rule, loved the Minotaur unreservedly, for he had told them all of his triumphs in the pantheon and had offered to adjudicate similar contests for a champion among their ranks.

The princes grew so concerned at the sway the Minotaur held in the empire that they tried several times to murder him. Once they sent two assassins to kill him in the chambers that the Empress had given him, but the Minotaur had grown so skilled at hearing during his years of blindness that he dispatched the men with ease. Next they tried poisoning his meals, but it had no effect upon him, even after they tripled the dosage. Stories of the failed attempts spread among the nobility and the Imperial Guard, and some began to wonder aloud if in fact he had been born of a god in his barbarian homeland.

The moment of his greatest triumph came years later, long after the Empress had secured her place upon the throne and thwarted the designs of the regent princes, imprisoning or exiling them so that she alone held sway in Huiam. The Minotaur felt happier than he ever had in all his days. The populace of Huiam worshiped him as they had in Rheadd at the height of his triumphs and, though the nobility and other grandees were bitterly jealous of his position, they dared not do anything to him for fear of incurring the Empress' wrath. All that he had ever longed for in his childhood in Guthril, suffering under the yoke of Thurir Drahil, was now his. The Empress neither worshiped him nor feared him; of all the people he had known she treated him a man worthy of respect.

It was into this idyll that Barthil Dethcallan Barthil arrived, an Emissary of Auten the Many-Fingered, sent to explore the possibility of trade and alliance with the Empire of Huiam, whose renown had reached the walls of Colosi. When the emissary was ushered before the court and announced by the heralds, the Minotaur nearly laughed aloud. To be face to face with this artifact of his past, his uncle no less, who had been a child when the Minotaur had ruled the pantheon, was a delight beyond his imagining. Fate, it seemed, had handed him the opportunity for some measure of revenge against those who had wronged him.

The Minotaur's pleasure would have increased infinitely had he been able to see Barthil Barthil's expression when his eyes settled upon him. The emissary could scarcely believe what he was seeing, for it surpassed all reason that there could be another creature such as the Minotaur in all the world, much less so one that had also been blinded. Word had reached Colosi of the Minotaur's rise and downfall in Alari and, when no more was heard of him, most had simply assumed that those savage barbarians had put an end to their former god, much to the delight of the Dethcalla. In the intervening years the family had succeeded in rehabilitating their standing in the empire, removing by threat and reward all mention of the creature from chronicles being written of the age. Already, with so many new champions in the pantheon, his memory among the populace was fading, and given time it seemed assured that he would be forgotten. Instead, the heir to Barthil Vulgih found himself face to face with the creature his father had seen banished and blinded.

"Welcome, Emissary," the Empress said after Barthil Barthil had regained his senses and abased himself before her. "It is a pleasure to meet another of your fine race. You no doubt recall the Champion of your pantheon, my Companion."

"It is an honor to be in your eternal presence, most exalted," Barthil Barthil said. He did not trust himself to say more, or to look at the Minotaur, for fear that he would betray his thoughts. To travel across the known world only to be faced by the very creature who had so stained his family's reputation – it was hard not to believe that the gods were mocking him.

"What brings you to our fair realm, Emissary?"

"I speak for Auten the Many-Fingered, the Emperor of Rheadd, who wishes that our two great empires be joined in eternal friendship."

"A weighty request. Emissary," the Empress said as the Minotaur whispered something to her ear.

Barthil Barthil winced at that. "I know that it is, most exalted. That is why I have been entrusted to bring you his proposals, as well as many gifts. Treasures the likes of which you have not seen in Huiam."

"I find that unlikely," the Empress said. "I already possess the singular treasure of your empire: my dear friend and Companion, Minotaur."

Barthil Barthil swallowed the bile that threatened to rise in his throat. "I promise you greater things than that await you, if you but allow me to show you, most exalted. I have—"

She did not allow him to finish. "You do not even acknowledge your nephew, Emissary?"

"He is the ruin of our family." Barthil Barthil could not stop himself from saying the words.

"So he shall be," the Empress said. "Go back to Rheadd and tell your Auten the Many-Fingered that Huiam is closed to his subjects on penalty of death until such time as the Dethcalla exist no longer."

The color drained from Barthil Barthil's face at those words, and he began to tremble violently. He could not return home with news such as this. He wanted to stay, to dispute the Empress' word somehow, though it was futile, he knew. The Minotaur had had his revenge upon their family and upon the Empire and he was helpless to stop it. It took all the strength he had to abase himself before the Empress one last time and leave the Eternal Palace to begin his journey home.

•••

Rheadd was never to recover from the blow delivered it by the Empress, the denial of the knowledge and trade of Huiam leading it into obscurity and poverty. Auten the Many-Fingered proved to be the last of his line, and in the years that followed much of the empire's territory was overrun by barbarians. Though Barthil Barthil had hidden the Empress' true reasons for closing Huiam to Rheadd, the Dethcalla were still blamed for the terrible fall the Empire suffered. In the violence and retribution that followed the end of Auten's rule, the leading members of the family, including an aged Barthil Vulgih, were all killed.

Huiam prospered under the long reign of the Empress, and by the end of her days all agreed that she had been a fine and just ruler. She had also resisted all suitors, remaining unmarried to her final days, with the result that she had no heir. As suitors had previously lined up to earn her hand, now claimants to the throne emerged from the great families of Huiam, seeking to gain her favor. As always, she was very careful in her dealings with the nobility, refusing to favor anyone, with the result that no one dared to act against their rivals or her for fear of ruining their chances of being proclaimed heir.

She kept up this game till her death, which came suddenly one afternoon as she and the Minotaur played a game of tiles. One moment she was triumphantly placing a tile and celebrating her victory, and the next her eyes had gone still and the breath had left her body. The Minotaur had taken her gently in his arms, trying to coax her back to life, to no avail. His sorrow at her passing was overwhelming. In the days that followed he ate and slept little, and took to wandering the halls at all hours, muttering to himself in a half-waking state. At times it seemed he thought she was still there with him.

The Imperial Guard, protectors of the Empress, saw to the funeral and his care, for he was seen as part of the imperial body. Given his fragile state of mind, no one wanted to disturb him, so when the Empress' body was set out in the greatest hall of the Eternal Palace – in fact, the very hall where the Doctor had first presented the Minotaur to the Empress – to remain in state for a fortnight, the Minotaur was brought to stand vigil over her. There he remained for the two weeks as important personages from across the empire came to pay their respects, oblivious to the internecine struggles occurring throughout the palace as various factions battled for who was to become the next ruler of Huiam. He did not notice the distance with which everyone now held him as well, or if he did he dismissed it as the reserve that always overcame those who approached someone in mourning. The days passed in a fog that would not lift, with all desire and emotion absent from his soul.

When the vigil was at end, the Empress' body was taken from the Eternal Palace to be interred in the sacred Valley of the Emperors outside Adaher. There were temples dedicated to each of the deceased emperors, where their remains, along with their personal treasure and keepsakes, were stored in massive crypts filled with warrens of passageways hidden beneath the earth. The Empress had begun construction on her temple and crypt as soon as she had claimed her throne, and it had been completed and had priests at the ready for over thirty years.

Now these men blessed and anointed her body and possessions and took them into the crypt under the watchful gaze of the assembled nobility. The treasure was staggering: gold and silver, jewelry and coins, as well as sculptures and statues of the Empress herself. Miniature forms of her Imperial Guard were placed within to protect her wealth on her journey to the afterworld. All that she had been in life was represented below, but for the Minotaur.

When the priests had completed their work and were ready to seal the tomb, the Imperial Guard surrounded the Minotaur, drawing their swords. Hearing that awakened him for the first time since the Empress' death, and he understood with a terrible clarity what was about to occur. He struggled against the Guard, crying in rage and anguish, and was bloodied by their weapons, before the strength and will at last went out of him and he submitted. He went below under the unmoving gaze of those assembled and the tomb was sealed above him. He gave one last cry, heard by all those gathered, cursing them and promising death and vengeance in this life or the next.

That done, he turned from the now-sealed entrance and went to sit beside the Empress' body for the days that remained to him.

EXCERPT:

REALM OF SHADOWS
VOLUME ONE OF THE SHADOW MEN

Craitol and Renuih, two empires a world apart, divided by the desert that lies between them. A desert ruled by the Shadow Men.

An uneasy peace holds sway in both realms, hiding longstanding feuds and bitter rivalries. Until a Shadow Men raid on Renuih shatters the calm and sets in motion events no one can control.

Masiph id Ezern, unfavored son of the Imperial Vazeir, finds himself a hero following the raid. His father remains unmoved by his exploits and, in his bitterness, Masiph will find himself a reluctant participant in a plot against the empire.

As he finds himself drawn deeper and deeper into the conspiracy, he soon realizes there will be no escaping the realm of shadows, where intrigue and betrayal abound. And though the Shadow Men have gone quiet, they will not stay silent forever...

1

Clouds blanketed the sky, rippling bruises in the twilight. The city Darrhyn below, sprawling along the bend of a wide river, was draped in the resultant shadows, pierced only intermittently by the remnants of the day's sun. Hurried figures passed from street to street in certain of its quarters to light the lamps, while others were left to what the night would bring. Along the city's great wall the beacons in the towers were struck, signaling the changing of the Watch. The new quadras marched up tower stairs, the soldiers heading out to pace the ramparts, looking into the final glare of the sun as it cast the scrub of the desert in oranges and reds.

Within one of the watchtowers five men squinted in the lamplight at a just-overturned cup, none of them speaking. Above them the sentinel on duty was singing an academy song about a woman so light in her manners that she would invite any man to sup with her.

"Call," the dealer said as he removed his hand from the cup, its contents still a mystery.

The youth to his left exhaled slowly as he eyed the cup. "Even. Five kenir," he said, the flames of the beacon above them snapping as more oil was added.

"Odd. I'll see you, Husem," the man beside him said, and the youth grimaced. "You're too young to be a gamester, I think."

He had a face gone thick with age and a long scar that ran from his chin up to his ear, just above the line of his jaw on one side. When he grinned, as he was doing now, it had the effect of creating what seemed a double smile on that half of his face.

"He lacks ability," the dealer said.

"Short on talent as well," the man said, to the laughter of everyone but the youth. The others at the table followed through with their bets, all odd.

Masiph id Ezern bit his lip. "I hope this is all above board," he said, staring at the dealer whose hand had strayed back to the cup.

"I hope so too," the man, Achelluth, said. "Someone short on talent and without ability certainly can't handle the underboard of life."

Masiph bit his lip again, not replying, and the dealer pulled the cup away, revealing two dice—a four and a three. There were whoops from around the table, but he did not look up, his eyes fixed on the dull bones whose pips had betrayed him again.

"That's it. I'm out," he said, pushing the last of his coins across the table. "I'm getting some air."

"Neither the coin nor the stamp for it, Husem," Achelluth called out, the white of his scar almost gleaming. "You haven't run through your allowance already, have you?"

"Hardly. I have better things to spend it on than at this table."

"Well, at least you are wise enough to know you will be spending it here," Achelluth said to more laughter. Masiph just nodded and walked out the door.

He wandered from the tower, stopping just outside the glow of the beacon to lean against the ramparts. It had been a cool day, given the rains could not be far away, and now that the sun was nearly set the night brought a chill. One of the two men on patrol on this stretch of the wall passed by, and they greeted each other. Masiph reached into the folds of his robe for the pouch that held his aslyn and put a quid in his cheek.

"Quiet night," he said, as the soldier passed back in the other direction.

"Every cursed night is quiet, Husem."

Masiph smiled, starting to work at the quid, as he stared idly at the veil of the night descending upon the desert. Here, so near the Eresnan River, it was a green desert—the short grass and sage brush that was its hallmark, plentiful and vibrant in color and scent. Once the rains began there would be even more as other plants began to flower. It was something he was curious to see, for though he had lived in Darrhyn his entire life he, like so many others from the city, had not set foot outside the western wall. When he had travelled it had been east into the Ferryen Plains, or down the Eresnan where the desert, so near, was safely kept from sight by the trees that lined its banks. To most Darrhynna, the desert was worthy of no more than a wary glance to the west and a scuff of a boot heel at the earth when talk turned to the Shadow Men.

Masiph had joined the Watch at the beginning of the dry season, five months ago, over his father's objections. For once Ibrazol had relented, though it had not felt like a victory as Masiph had expected. It felt like his father had in some way outmaneuvered him again, achieving his desired end in allowing his son this. Perhaps he had. Masiph never could tell what his father's thoughts were and was still not clear on his own feelings now that he had achieved his desire. The work itself was tedious—a few weeks on, a few days off, and always a quiet night.

This in spite of what one could hear walking the streets. To listen to the talk there was to believe that the Imperial city's very existence was precarious, given its location in that nebulous region near the Empire's border where the desert began. And the desert was the Shadows' domain. Never mind that the Shadow Men, even as they were conquering the desert, shattering the Empire a hundred years ago, had never dared an attack on Darrhyn and its fabled great walls. None had in the five centuries it had served as capital of Renuih.

There had been a raid a week ago in Fardun, little more than a day's journey southeast—the first of the season, and earlier than usual, given the rains had not started. Strangely, the fact that it was an unimportant farming village seemed to lead to even more anguish among the populace. There was no sense to it, but why did there have to be? It was the Shadows, after all. They were without reason and purpose, moving like common beasts with the seasons, content with the barest of existences on the rock and scrub of the desert.

In the streets talk turned to conspiracy and invasion. This was the only tangible result of a Shadow Men raid. That afternoon Masiph had heard that the shadows were gathering near Ghehel and were working to rebuild the Nasuila Bridge to use as a gateway to strike at the heart of the Empire, cutting the Ferryen Plains off from the capital and the southern provinces. At any given moment in the rainy season Darrhyn was a day or hours away from a massive army of the Shadows materializing at its gates. In a week, maybe less, it would all be forgotten—until word of the next attack arrived.

We live in an age diminished, Masiph thought, *the shadows of greater days*. Before the fall of the desert, even during that desperate struggle to maintain their hold in that realm, the denizens of this city would never have cowered at the mention of a mere raid by the Shadows. The thought would have been laughable. Now those who had to memorize their invocations, and even some of their betters, spoke of the Shadow Men as the natural inhabitants of the desert. Generations of Renians had known no other life but that of the desert—and that included his own family—yet that seemed to be almost forgotten now, or at least dismissed.

"What's the thought this evening?" Nustef id Illied said to him as he stepped out of the tower. The Nohritai was older than his fellow nobleman, with narrow features and a heavier green tone to his skin than was usual for those from Darrhyn.

"We can only bear a life of fear so long," Masiph said.

"Heavy things indeed, especially for someone with no marrow in his bones," Nustef laughed.

"Where else do you find the pox but in the bones?"

"The voice of experience, perhaps? Are you preparing lines for your chronicle?"

"I don't think so. The historians just put whatever words they want into the mouths of whoever anyway. Husem Azyereh was illiterate, I've been told."

"Really?"

"Yes. He was not a favored cousin."

More laughter. "Fair enough, I suppose. I always forget that he had a life before he became the Ad Eselte's Vazeir."

"Someday though," Masiph said, "we'll have to do something about the shadows or we'll be nothing more than carrion for them to feast on. Better to act now than to be put to the squeak later."

"You shouldn't listen to what you hear in the drinkeries. It only bothers the blood."

"The drink or the talk?" he said.

"I wouldn't know these things. I lead a pious life, as my ancestors and the sage Delth proscribe."

Masiph spat over the wall in response and Nustef smiled. "Talk to Our Most Benevolent One. Don't you have his ear by now?"

"Oh yes, I join him daily for his constitutionals and we discuss all the important matters of the Empire in between verses."

"Does he really go walking about every morning?"

Masiph shrugged. I would be the last to know.

Nustef took his own quid out, putting it in his cheek, and the two of them chewed in silence. There was a small copse near the wall that was filled with dahrrynna birds, the capital's namesake, and their animated calls as they roused themselves for an evening of feasting on insects drowned the air. This was the scene that faced them every night as the sun slipped below the horizon, and that familiarity and the calm that now settled over the day's end was seductive.

Masiph felt strongly about what he said regarding the Shadows. It was an easy thing to be passionate about, given no one was so derelict of their senses as to invade the desert. A byproduct of the restlessness of youth, his father would say in that dismissive tone which burned his ears. That his father, and no doubt that useless philosopher Ad Eselte, frowned upon his views only served to confirm them even more firmly in his mind. Something would have to be done, if only because no one else seemed to think that was the case.

The last Renian force to invade the desert in an attempt to reclaim their birthright had been led by a cousin of his father's, Waleen, ten years before his own birth. Two hundred sons, the flower of the Darrhynna youth, had joined him, dazzled by his speeches calling for a crusade to purify the desert of the black scourge, to resurrect those ancestors lost there and restore the empire whole. The result was predictable: a laughable disaster guided by a mad fool. Most failed to return and those who did were ruined, never to be whole again. Masiph had seen a few of them on visits to other Nohritai homes, balding men who walked about like children, unsure of each step.

Such a catastrophe had the effect of ensuring that no Ad Eselte or Nohritai would propose a war against the Shadow Men for generations. Still, Masiph admired Waleen his madness. His cousin, he thought, probably had felt much as he did the echo in each step of his life. If a cauldron of blood in the desert was necessary to drag this plain into a new age, then let it come.

"He's a poet," he said, breaking their silence. "He has the pouting lips for squeaking after all. Certainly no stomach for war."

"Probably he's too concerned about self-important Nohritai who think they know better than him how to run the empire." Nustef said.

A clanging bell, not far down the wall, stifled Masiph's reply. They both looked at each other, not quite believing what they were hearing. It was an alarm. Darrhyn, first city of the Empire, was under attack.

REALM OF SHADOWS is the first volume in the epic fantasy trilogy THE SHADOW MEN.

ABOUT THE AUTHOR

Clint Westgard is the author of The Shadow Men Trilogy and the science fiction epic The Sojourner Cycle, the first volume of which, The Forgotten, was published in 2015. In addition, he has published a work of historical fantasy set in colonial Peru, The Maleficio Chronicles, and a retelling of the Minotaur legend, The Trials of the Minotaur. Clint Westgard lives in Calgary, Alberta.

ALSO BY CLINT WESTGARD

Realm of Shadows
Volume One of The Shadow Men

Craitol and Renuih, two empires a world apart, divided by the desert that lies between them. A desert ruled by the Shadow Men.

An uneasy peace holds sway in both realms, hiding longstanding feuds and bitter rivalries. Until a Shadow Men raid on Renuih shatters the calm and sets in motion events no one can control.

Masiph id Ezern, unfavored son of the Imperial Vazeir, finds himself a hero following the raid. His father remains unmoved by his exploits and, in his bitterness, Masiph will find himself a reluctant participant in a plot against the empire.

As he finds himself drawn deeper and deeper into the conspiracy, he soon realizes there will be no escaping the realm of shadows, where intrigue and betrayal abound. And though the Shadow Men have gone quiet, they will not stay silent forever...

ALSO BY CLINT WESTGARD

Council of Shadows
Volume Two of The Shadow Men

Discontent continues to fester within the realms of Craitol
and Renuih, fed by intrigues carried out in the shadows. As
rivals and apostates struggle for supremacy, a long
incubated plan begins to unfold.

Vyissan, a mysterious alkemycal practitioner arrives in
Renuih, the latest strike in a long war over who shall
control the secrets of alkemya and Craitol itself. He carries
with him a secret that, once revealed, will reverberate
across all realms. Before he can reveal it though, the
conspirators against the emperor will strike their own
blow.

But now, a new and more powerful menace looms on the
horizon. The Shadow Men have gained the secrets of the
Council Adept's alkemya and no one can be certain what
they will do with it…

ALSO BY CLINT WESTGARD

Dance of Shadows
Volume Three of The Shadow Men

War with the Shadow Men looms in both realms as the
consequences of the Gvers' Council in Craitol begin to
make themselves known. A war that could end in glorious
triumph or bitter disaster.

Doubt shadows everyone's steps, for they know there are
no certainties in the desert. Especially now the Shadow
Men have made the art of alkemya their own.

No one has more questions than Vyissan, for he is
working in service to a cause he is no longer sure he
believes in. And now he must undertake a journey with
those who both loathe and fear him. Before the first sword
is drawn, his life will be under threat.

But his will not be the only one, for somewhere in the
desert the Shadow Men lie in wait…

ALSO BY CLINT WESTGARD

The Forgotten
Volume One of The Sojourners Cycle

Who is David Aeida? And what does he know that has so
many people pursuing him?

David doesn't know. He can't remember anything about
who he is. But he finds himself ensnared in a vicious
conflict between a religious cult and a guild that patrols the
crossings between multiple universes. They will both stop
at nothing to gain whatever knowledge he possesses. Most
dangerous of all, is the implacable hunter, known only as
the Seeker, who has his own reasons for wanting to find
David.

His only hope is to recover his memories before they do.
His only ally is a woman named Meredith, and she
definitely knows more than she is telling...

Spanning both universes and the human mind, The
Forgotten is an unforgettable science fiction thriller that
questions the very nature of identity. It is the first volume
of the Sojourners Cycle, an epic that will encompass the
fates of universes and humanity itself.

ALSO BY CLINT WESTGARD

The Apostate
Volume Two of The Sojourners Cycle

Laila has only one goal in mind. To have her revenge upon the Grand Regent for all he has done to her. First, though, she needs to find her way across the universes.

That is easier said than done. The Grand Regent's agents are still pursuing her. As is the Society of Travellers. And the Seeker lurks somewhere, waiting for his moment to strike.

Laila has a plan, though, and a few tricks of her own. But she will discover that not everything is at seems. For the war she has given her life to hides a far greater conflict.

Spanning multiple universes and the complexities of the human mind, The Apostate, continues the incredible journey begun in The Forgotten. The second volume of The Sojourners Cycle is an unforgettable science fiction epic that encompasses the fates of universes and humanity itself.

ALSO BY CLINT WESTGARD

The Maleficio Chronicles

Luisa is always more than she appears. Rumor and mystery
surround her. And strange events seem to follow wherever
she goes.

Born in Lima, City of Kings, to a noble family, her father
so fears her true nature that he banishes her to a convent.
There she falls under the suspicion of the Inquisition and
decides to flee.

Disguised as a man, she embarks upon a series of wild
adventures, dueling, carousing, and gambling her way
across colonial Peru. But everything changes when
someone recognizes her for what she truly is, and soon she
finds herself fighting for her very survival.

In a world where she will always stand apart, Luisa
undergoes a strange journey, marked by betrayal and
murder, terrible powers and mysterious strangers. *The
Maleficio Chronicles* is her incredible confession and a story
like no other.

ALSO BY CLINT WESTGARD

The Devious Kind

A Mystery

The body of a local woman is found in a coulee on a ranch north of Loverna, her head blown off with a shotgun. New to town and the job, Constable Martin Thomas arrives on the scene as a spring snowstorm begins to wipe out all evidence before his investigation has even begun.

There is no shortage of suspects to consider. A spurned husband. A jealous lover. A betrayed business partner. And family members battling over an inheritance. All have motive and opportunity. And no one seems to be telling him everything.

As he tries to sift the truth from the lies, the snowstorm continues to build, leaving Loverna cut off from the outside world. And Thomas alone to face a killer who will do anything not to get caught.